THE EMPIRE
OF
ILLUSION

GLOBAL AFRICAN VOICES
Dominic Thomas, editor

AMINATA SOW FALL

THE EMPIRE
OF
ILLUSION

TRANSLATED BY MEG FURNISS WEISBERG

INDIANA UNIVERSITY PRESS

This book is a publication of

Indiana University Press
Office of Scholarly Publishing
Herman B Wells Library 350
1320 East 10th Street
Bloomington, Indiana 47405 USA

iupress.org

© 2018, Le Serpent à Plumes
© 2023 by Indiana University Press

Manufactured in the United
States of America

Cataloging information is available
from the Library of Congress.

ISBN 978-0-253-06699-2 (hardback)
ISBN 978-0-253-06700-5 (ebook)

First Printing 2023

To you, Cheikh Sadibou Fall
My brother
My friend
Your shield: faith
Your kingdom: wisdom
Incorruptible knight of virtue
All honor to you
Affection

PREFACE

Aminata Sow Fall is the uncontested matriarch of the French-language African socialist realist novel. Her 1976 novel *Le revenant* was the first written work of prose fiction published in French by a Black African woman. Others had published memoirs or other nonfictional works; *Le revenant* was the first to use the liberties and power of imagination and invention to give a "realer-than-real" picture of a social phenomenon. Her trenchantly satirical second novel, *La grève des bàttu / The Beggars' Strike* (1979, tr. Dorothy Blair, 1986), became—and continues to be—widely read. It was shortlisted for the prestigious Prix Goncourt and won the Grand prix littéraire d'Afrique noire, and it has been translated into several languages, including Chinese, Finnish, and Spanish. Cheick Oumar Sissoko made it into a film, *Bàttu*, in 2000, and it continues to figure prominently on syllabi and must-read lists internationally. While her second novel remains her best known, she's since written eight others and has received many other honors, including the Prix International Alioune Diop, the Grand Prix de la francophonie from the Académie française, and an honorary doctorate from Mount Holyoke College.

In other words, although the book you hold in your hands now may be slight, it is anything but lightweight. Although not what French-language readers usually call a *pavé* ("a cobblestone," meaning a huge and weighty book—think *War and Peace*), it is certainly another important brick in the path that Aminata Sow Fall is attempting to lead her readers down: a path toward "a world of humanity, respect, and dignity for every human being." Indeed, her approach to writing is a personal attempt to grapple with a societal question or observation that's troubling her and capturing her attention. In a 2014 interview with Jonathan Walsh for the journal *Women in French Studies*, she stated that she always writes "starting from a fundamental question. . . . It's simply that I dream of" the possibility of people being at their best.[1] Certainly a consequential undertaking, yet one it's easy to take with you in your backpack!

Although Aminata Sow Fall studied literature, it was never her express goal to become a writer. She completed her university and postgraduate studies in Paris at the Sorbonne and returned to Senegal after getting married, with the intention of pursuing a career as a teacher. After seven years abroad, she was shocked and unsettled by the changes she witnessed: "It seemed to me that the way of life had developed too fast. I no longer recognized some aspects of my own society, and one example of this struck me forcefully: it was the new power that money had acquired in people's relations with each other."[2] This led her to take up her pen and puzzle through what she observed by inventing characters who reflected and enacted what she was seeing. Far from being mere two-dimensional puppets that stand in for an abstract idea, the characters of all her

---

1. Jonathan Walsh, "Entretien avec Aminata Sow Fall," *Women in French Studies* 22 (2014): 87–96. My translation.
2. Peter Hawkins, "An Interview with Aminata Sow Fall," *African Affairs* 87, no. 348 (July 1988): 419–30.

novels are meant to actively manifest aspects of a philosophical question. Those descriptions might sound like the same thing, but I would argue there's an important difference: whereas the former is static, lifeless, and dogmatic, I see the latter as much more engaged and humane. We might call Aminata Sow Fall a philosopher in that her writing is primarily concerned with tackling huge, broad questions of humanity and society, but her philosophical approach is deeply rooted in an empathic connection to her fellow citizens of the world. Answering these questions only matters insofar as the answers help people live more fully and humanely.

This approach does mean that the novels don't always read like what many American readers are used to: the characters are often relatively flat because they are amalgams of a certain type; the plot doesn't always move in a predictably linear fashion; the story isn't full of adventure and doesn't follow what American schoolchildren are taught is "the" narrative arc. Médoune Guèye has pointed out that Aminata Sow Fall's work follows certain conventions of traditional folktales the world over, such as a dualistic approach or the structuring of the text as a semantic unit in order to convey a moral or message.[3] This seems like an important point for us as readers to bear in mind: different types of tales and texts follow different logics and have different goals. This is why her work is such a welcome addition to the Global African Voices series at Indiana University Press. Aminata Sow Fall's work escapes simple or even potentially reductive categorization: she cannot readily be essentialized or, for that matter, discounted or dismissed for discounting, dismissing, or even relinquishing accepted or perceived standards for novelistic production. Instead, she

3. Médoune Guèye, "Criticism, Écriture, and Orality in the African Novel: Oral Discourse in Aminata Sow Fall's Work," *Research in African Literatures* 45, no. 2 (Summer 2014): 86–102.

complicates the assessment and reception of her work. As Eileen Julien observes, reductionist interpretations "hold the novel hostage to the demands or expectations of a hegemonic readership"[4] and prevent us from engaging with the author's individual style.

Aminata Sow Fall is the first to explain that she does not employ particular literary devices, styles, or tactics "in a calculated way." She abhors the idea of writers "defining themselves in relation to others" and wants to write in "a natural, unselfconscious way." She notes that "you can't carry in yourself a whole heritage . . . without revealing it." Thus, her novels "carry with them a heritage of tradition, from folk-tales, from stories, from legends,"[5] all in service of grappling with fundamental questions. Her deepest wish for humanity is that we all combine what's best in the traditions available to us with whatever developments and advances come along to help guide us to the most natural expression of our inherent capacity for understanding and care; therefore, it makes sense that she would be as natural, unstudied, and true to herself as possible in her writing. As you read this book or any other by this author, remember that you're reading the work of an optimist, but one with no veil over her eyes, no rose-colored glasses. She, like James Baldwin, aims for acceptance without complacency, for the never-ending struggle against injustice borne from the belief that while injustice is a constant, the possibility of goodness is just as real.[6] Every one of Aminata Sow Fall's books is this particular philosopher-artist's subjective and imaginative attempt to answer a societal

---

4. Eileen Julien, "Reading 'Orality' in French-Language Novels from Sub-Saharan Africa," in *Francophone Postcolonial Studies: A Critical Introduction*, eds. Charles Forsdick and David Murphy (London: Routledge, 2003), 122–32.
5. Hawkins, "An Interview," 423.
6. James Baldwin, "Notes of a Native Son," in *The Art of the Personal Essay: An Anthology from the Classical Era to the Present*, ed. Phillip Lopate (New York: Anchor, 1995), 587–604.

question, and it's always apparent that she believes our humanity can pull us through.

The Empire of Illusion is no different. Its central question is,
"How does a person gain, earn, and keep respect?" Aminata
Sow Fall has said that there are certain words in Wolof that she
needs to leave in the original in her books because they are "key
words of our very way of life."[7] The word *jom* is one of those: the
basic translation would be "honor," and certainly many societ-
ies value honor highly. In her first novel, she took a satirical look
at how the idea of *jom* can get warped into ostentatious flaunt-
ing of wealth and status, only to pull a one-eighty and demon-
strate how a person can make huge sacrifices to safeguard the
family's honor. In her 1982 novel, *L'appel des arènes* (*The Call
of the Arenas*), Aminata Sow Fall explores the confrontation
and compromises that occur when two systems of *jom*/per-
sonal honor meet and mix. And now, this latest novel explores
some paths people can take to develop, earn, and keep—or
stray from and lose—their *jom*. Unlike some of her previous
books where the main characters themselves undergo various
moral failings and reversals (a typical structure in folktales of
all cultures), in this one, for the most part, the main characters
are all fundamentally moral and are trying to steer their tiny
ship of right conduct through the turbulent seas of a society
rife with crosscurrents of greed, pretension, self-promotion,
and a general lack of respect. Therein lies the question: What
and who deserves respect? Why do or don't they receive it in
today's society? And not only that, but how does someone cul-
tivate and maintain self-respect when surrounded by crass and
senseless unkindness or the pressure to conform to ethically
dubious norms?

---

7. Cristina Schiavone, "À propos de 'Le jujubier du patriarche': Entretien avec
Aminata Sow Fall," *Francofonia* 27 (Autumn 1994): 87–95. This quote, 88.

The Empire of Illusion has what one might call an ensemble cast: though the story of Sada Waar's family and childhood takes up the bulk of the narrative, it's safe to say that the bond between the main characters is in fact the lead. The novel begins with what Médoune Guèye describes as the "opening finale"— a vignette in which the central question is announced through a dramatic confrontation. At one of the family's regular Sunday gatherings, the usual postmeal *palabres* turn tense when Sada's adolescent son, Diéry, asks why his father was so buddy-buddy with a government official at a televised ribbon cutting the day before. Right from the start, the question of respect is examined in its many facets: Why do certain people get certain titles and honorifics? What are we doing when we use those titles? How does a person maintain self-respect when forced to swim in ethically muddy waters? What respect does a son owe his father—and vice versa? How does a family or any other collective unit maintain an equilibrium of debate and respect? And that's all just in the first scene! From there, the author takes us through vignettes from the pasts of various characters to accretively show how we got to that first-last scene, giving us her answer to these questions along the way.

Yes, Aminata Sow Fall gives answers. This is a didactic form. There's a moral to the story. That said, I would call it an invitational moral rather than a proscriptive one: I think the author sincerely hopes we will find ourselves in these characters, in their dilemmas, thus coming to the same conclusions the author draws about humanity's capacity for respect and the choices that will most likely lead toward or away from that respect.

The title—*L'empire du mensonge* in the original, which I've translated as *The Empire of Illusion*—is multilayered, a clue to the novel's central problem and to the antidote it proposes. It hints at the different forms of deception and untruth practiced by various authorities, governmental or otherwise, which our ensemble cast must learn to confront, evade, upend, or stare down. It also offers a solution. One of our ensemble, Borso, is an actor and playwright as well as an outspoken social critic, and she names her new cultural center the Empire of Illusion, nodding ironically to an aspect of fiction and all artistic and creative production—its inherent opposition to and escape from reality—both to create a space where free expression reigns supreme (thus, "Empire") and to turn the weapon of manipulating reality back on those who would wield it for corrupt purposes.

Many critics and scholars have explored the concept of orality as an element in African novelistic production, and by that term they mean a variety of things: cadences in written dialogue or narration that reflect speech patterns; references, in both content and form, to African storytelling traditions; the use of proverbs; an interspersing of words in other languages. We could find all of these things in this novel, though the author herself would caution us against making assumptions about her intentional deployment of these literary strategies. "Culture and tradition don't want to be stuck," she says: "I claim what's best in my tradition [but] I don't systematically seek to use [these elements] in my writing. When this sort of thing shows up naturally on its own while I'm writing, I don't hesitate because it mustn't be artificial."[8] To Sow Fall, the influences of culture and tradition are often absorbed without our necessarily even realizing it's happening, only to surface in our lives and work in refracted or unexpected ways. In the novel, we're offered a metanarrative reflection on one of the female characters' spontaneous gestures of strong defense: "Did Sabou know the epic of those valiant heroines who, one way

8. Walsh, "Entretien," 92, 94 (my translation).

or another, in times of peace, war, or catastrophe, wrote the most beautiful lines in Humanity's story?" Whatever aspects of "orality" appear in this novel, the author, like the character Sabou, is writing her story as it spontaneously arises. It naturally includes elements of her interpretive framework, though she would deny she's consciously invoking any aspect of oral literature in particular in her stylistic choices.

Like any novel worth its salt, *The Empire of Illusion* is both intensely rooted in its environment and universally accessible. Aminata Sow Fall believes "it's a false idea to try to write for others [because] if you do, you're compromising your own sincerity."[9] While she doesn't have a particular audience in mind, this and her other works are deeply anchored in contemporary Senegal, even when set in cities or regions the author herself doesn't know well. That said, the author repeatedly makes a point of underscoring the universality of the questions she ponders and the experiences of her characters and the nonpartisan aspect of humanism: "If being committed means that one is concerned . . . that the great problems that confront our countries, our continent, our world even, are all our own problems, then I would say that I am a committed writer." The universal through the lens of an author's subjectivity is what Aminata Sow Fall sees as literature's contribution "because when other people write, and discover themselves, they leave us to discover them for ourselves, to see for ourselves who they are."[10]

9. Hawkins, "An Interview," 422.
10. Hawkins, "An Interview," 422–23.

THE EMPIRE
OF
ILLUSION

IN THE DINING ROOM, at the other end of the living room: the area gives off a pleasant air of calm and happiness. A scent of lavender, a harmony of colors: very light beige walls, acacia wood furniture, moldings in beige and ocher mosaic tiles. From the ceiling, a magic lantern spreads a soft light to the four corners of the vast room. Refinement and simplicity.

Sundays at 2:00 p.m. sharp for the past fifteen years.

Yacine has finished simmering her gombo and palm oil sauce. *Soupe kandia* this Sunday, as only she knows how to make it—like an inspired artist. She is glowing. The joy of a foodie, for sure. But, above all, a passion long cultivated around the cooking hearth of Yaaye Diodio, her deceased mother, who brought to the culinary arts and to mealtime a considerable, even mystical, reverence. From a very young age, Yacine had thus learned to cook out of love, absorbing the secrets without feeling like she'd been learning.

Enticing smells perfume the atmosphere. The core of the "Sunday crowd" is already settled in. Sada, of course, Yacine's happy husband; Diéry, the gifted teen, the couple's pride and joy and the apple of his aunt Borso's eye; Coumba, Yacine's close friend and a full-fledged family member because Yaaye Diodio and her husband, Uncle Fara Diaw, had been welcoming her over since her tender childhood; and finally, Boly and Mignane, Sada's childhood friends, the truest of the true. Others will come: old acquaintances, close or distant relatives, neighbors. They won't lack for food or shelter. All united in the assurance of sharing a moment of communion and rest.

Everyone is waiting for Borso, Yacine's twin. She sent a message to her sister's phone: "I'll be there in about 15 minutes."

Thirty minutes. Coumba calls to Yacine: "You know perfectly well that for Borso, the time is never a set thing!" Turning to the others, she adds, her fingers pointing to the dining room: "The meal is ready."

Complicit silence. Everyone approves but doesn't dare say so. "And besides, why wait? It's self-serve. Even if she shows up at five p.m., there'll still be something in the belly of these big tureens." Putting her words into action, she gets up. Straight for the dining room.

"That's you all over!" says Yacine, smiling.

"Yeah, that's me," responds Coumba, heading away, the core of the "Sunday crowd" behind her. "That's me! Borso's not going to lay down the law here. You know she'll put on a big scene for us. Diéry will applaud and give her a kiss on the cheek. She'll calm down. No one will bring up how late she was."

Everyone dives in. Perfect conviviality. In unison, warm compliments for Yacine. She is more than a little proud to honor her mother's memory by perpetuating a tradition of joy and sharing that once gave meaning to her existence. Yacine is in heaven, and no one can doubt it, even if her legendary restraint clears her from any hint of vanity. They can see it in her gaze that speaks volumes with its light and in that discreet smile that brightens her face. Yaaye Diodio's coppery voice resonates in her heart. "Mealtime . . . a sacred celebration . . . thanks to God . . . the salutary flight of human beings back into the universe of their original purity . . . jubilation . . . the feast of the soul." And more words still to say that food is not simply a matter of the belly. This strong conviction punctuated Yaaye Diodio's almost incantatory remarks when, in the big courtyard of the family home swept by the Ocean's breezes, she had finished offering a feast to those who were lucky enough to savor her talents and her generosity. From time to time, a voice would bubble up like a magic potion and set the tone for a polyphonic chorus of lyrical compliments that would fill the atmosphere before fading into the rush of waves a few meters from the house. Dance steps would stir up the fine sand into a cloud of raucous excitement that filled the courtyard to the joy of all those present.

In all modesty, Yacine knows she can't equal Yaaye Diodio. She doesn't even have that ambition anyway, or the pretention. Still, after many years spent abroad and despite her professional obligations that grant her no respite, one day she firmly resolved to devote Sundays to cooking. A wonderful chance to recreate the enlivening atmosphere of her childhood and reconnect with this "sacred celebration" that she so missed. And also, it must be said, to satisfy her own unbridled love of good food. Yaaye Diodio had intended food to be good "in beauty, quality, and abundance," and Yacine had certainly taken up that motto, though you'd never know it from her near-perfect body. Very quickly, she then discovered without having really thought about it that the "burden" of cooking, royally scorned by Coumba, has the gift of drowning her day-to-day stress in the delicious, steamy vapors that rise from her cooking pots.

Euphoria, for sure. Right up until Diéry gets the idea to tease his father. "Hey, Dad, yesterday, at the groundbreaking for the International University of Excellence, I was so surprised! I saw it on TV. I said, 'Look at that! There's Dad showering

Macoumba with so much praise.' Even offering him the title
His Excellency."

"It was definitely surprising," breaks in Yacine with that convincing ponderousness that characterizes her.

Boly keeps it going: "Our son is right! Sada, why? I'd planned
on bringing up the question today to liven up teatime. Frankly,
Macoumba doesn't deserve those compliments from you! That
filthy liar doesn't believe in anything. Listening to the TV yesterday, you'd think the two of you still hang out. How long
has it been since you last saw him?" Then, laughing, he added,
"Yesterday, he was on his fiftieth groundbreaking." Laughter
from the whole crowd, except Sada.

"It's true!" insists Boly. "Fifty groundbreakings in twelve
years of flip-flopping and ministry hopping—"

"You mean nomadism, Uncle?" says Diéry.

"Say it like that if you want. You're young—that's the style
these days." Frank laughter again. Sada remains impenetrable.

"Hospitals, clinics, schools! Wherever people feel least at
ease," continues Boly. "Up to this day, nothing at all. Today,
the International University of Excellence. Those people sure
know how to fetishize words."

"Uncle!" Diéry tosses out again. "Fifty in twelve years isn't
really excessive! Less than five per year."

"Go tell that to the poor communities. I wrote it down in my
little notebook. Reflex of an old, outmoded teacher, maybe. To
hold out against the generalized amnesia that's paralyzing our
spirits and turning us into robots. Fifty grandiose happenings
for vain applause—paid for dearly and nothing at all for the
people. All this time, schools have ended up crumbling down
and hospitals have collapsed on the heads of penniless patients.
And it just keeps going."

Coumba cut him off short. "Listen, Boly, your speech on 'the
people' . . . you sound like the same people you're pointing a
finger at."

"Exactly, but I at least stay true to myself."

"*Ey*, buddy! That was back in the good old days. How much of yourself have you got left?" A concert of laughter. Mignane, the sage of the group, nods his head.

Boly picked back up: "Sada, I was more than surprised to see you there yesterday!" One by one, Mignane, Coumba, Yacine—again—took off in the same conversational direction.

Sada listened to them with a heavy heart, of course; his face was serious. Vexed deep down. Nevertheless, he forced a smile.

Silence. Then: "You're all right."

Nodding his head, he continued: "I shouldn't have done it. I shouldn't have. It's true. Macoumba really pressured me to attend that ceremony. Invitation card, repeated telephone calls. Evoking our childhood. Our pranks. Our stupid mistakes. Our joys too! In the thick of the hustle, of precarity . . . and violence sometimes, right before our eyes. Our luck at having escaped the traps of that unforgiving milieu . . . and the luck of having become what we are now, thanks to our parents' vigilance."

Silence.

"Doubtless, that's how he really touched me. Yes, he touched me. This International University of Excellence project got a ton of financing from foreign lenders; it's targeting youth from disadvantaged areas. Macoumba was counting on my presence and that of the other guests I didn't know. A manner of demonstrating via examples at hand that the 'poverty trap' doesn't exist. It lines up with my convictions, you all know it. I thought I could give hope to the hundred or so young people who were there and who no doubt dreamed of an enviable future."

A good solid minute charged with emotion. Coumba couldn't help but exclaim with indignation: "They tricked you! That cretin and his cronies are only interested in the financing; they don't care at all about those young people! Just like before, they'll siphon off the cash with no guilty conscience. They've got no heart. It's horrible. Hens will have teeth before those people become honest! And the money from previous projects?"

Silence.

Maybe a little ripple of despair in the hearts of some people.

Still no sign of Borso. The grilling session comes to an end. It's part of their usual routine, following an unwritten resolution they've chosen to impose on themselves for many years: to get themselves collectively back on track each time as necessary if one or the other of them derails the conversation, according to their own terms. Not to hurt or to humiliate. Anything but a courtroom trial. A lucid and courageous act, an exercise in mental hygiene in order to escape the conformism of all the illusion, the lying, the denunciations, and the hypocrisy that had ended up poisoning the national atmosphere and inhibiting everyone's conscience.

The freshness of mint in the air. A signal of the first round of *ataya*, that voluptuous tea that, like a sacrament, must close out mealtime by sealing everyone's hearts with the symbol of the kind of true fraternity that is exemplary, sincere, and generous.

Everyone's nostrils are pleased. Diéry is thinking again of the term *excellence* that's been bugging him more and more. He's determined to pick it apart once and for all and to permanently clear up the usage of the expression *His Excellency.* "To whom should we attribute the title His Excellency?"

To Sada, the question was like a bludgeon to the head. He suddenly blew his top after a long silence, cutting off Boly, who was already ready to revisit the list of precedence. "Listen, Diéry, cut it out! That's enough, already!"

Diéry is surprised. The whole crowd understood that his question was innocent, in the context of the sorts of discussions, rumpuses, and interrogations his father had accustomed him to, often in the presence and with the participation of the group. They all loved that—they could get into a heated and noisy grammatical battle over the placement of a comma in a phrase or the use of the relative pronoun *whom* that was getting more and more massacred, to the dismay of the purists, or over Black people's capacity to philosophize. It was a way of playing for them, with absolutely no pretense of displaying erudition. Among other things, as well, a means for Sada to build between his son and himself a relationship of confidence, tenderness, and moving complexity. He thought he could thus develop his son's abilities to reflect and to analyze, leading him to understand what was at stake in our world and to choose his path, with total freedom, in dignity. And in perfect compatibility with the norms of respect, restraint, and sociability. Diéry's precocious intelligence had encouraged him. And also, that exquisite civility that demanded admiration and sympathy even before the boy had hit seventeen.

Sada got up brusquely. Visibly worked up, which was rare. His right index finger pointed at Diéry. His voice hoarse. "Don't overstep your bounds! Who do you think you are, you pretentious person! Are you my censor to go digging around in my smallest words and gestures in order to catch me out in some dishonoring slipup! I am neither a liar nor a hypocrite, much less a flunky. You're well placed to know it!"

Pause. Silence all around. Then, with a calmer tone: "If I stuck that title on Macoumba after the rest of the people up there on the grandstand with me did, lining myself up with them without thinking . . . is that a reason to stick me in the pillory?"

Petrified crowd. No one dares intervene, to avoid poisoning the situation any further. Everyone has absorbed the essential unwritten lesson inscribed on the immaterial tablets of their heritage. *Wox du forox*, said the sage: speech doesn't ferment.[1] Know how to listen and not to speak until the opportune moment.

Diéry's head is bowed. No expression on his face. Unhappy down to the very depths of his being. Sada, still visibly moved, paternal: "Diéry. I'm the one who dragged you onto the field of free discussion. My dream is that you will be a free man and proud. This dream of honesty that we all share here, along with Borso, who's made it her incessant battle cry . . ."

Sada didn't finish his sentence. The looks on everyone's faces made him sense that something was happening. He turned his head. Ten feet away, there was Borso! Standing up. She'd missed almost none of Sada's speech while she'd been coming along the flowered veranda that runs outside the room's doors and windows.

"Oh, Borso! Hello," stuttered Sada, holding out a trembling hand.

"Hello, Sada," responded Borso, impenetrable and rigid as a statue. "Hello, everyone."

Everyone frozen, including Boly, the eternal chatterbox and hairsplitter. They'd all understood that they needed to let Sada get his bitterness out and hold off on patching things up.

"It's only human," Mignane said to himself. "It can happen that we explode sometimes, right or wrong."

Sada went back to his spot. Crushed to the very depths of his flesh not only for having lost his temper at Diéry but for having made a spectacle of himself, even if only in front of family and friends. Between him and Borso there had never been a single

---

1. Translator's note: Throughout the text, Aminata Sow Fall uses phrases and proverbs in Wolof and then gives a gloss or explanation in French. I have translated the author's French-language explanations rather than seeking to translate directly from the Wolof; thus, any discrepancies between the Wolof phrase and the English explanation arise from this intermediate step.

cloud. Beyond the affection and familiarity that links them like joking cousins, he feels a profound respect for her. For how deeply he esteems her, for her rigor and her integrity. For the fact that he owes her respect as his sister-in-law. For her goodness and the contagious gaiety that she spreads wherever she goes, especially at their house, where she's set up her weekend headquarters to be around the beautiful eyes of Diéry, whom she calls *sama taaw*, "my own oldest son," ever since the day she plucked him from Yacine's belly on the sparkling dawn of a stormy night, in a little hamlet deep in the forest, without a hospital or any form of medical assistance. Sada had been working a modest gold-mining plot bitterly snatched from the voracity of all those foreign investors comfortably installed in their gated compounds, where they were insulated from the small-time gold panners who'd come from all over and far removed from the local citizens, who were deprived of almost everything.

Yacine hadn't hesitated to join Sada there when she was in an advanced state of pregnancy. She'd completely ignored the warnings and the risks of such a dangerous trip in an area where she didn't know anyone. Was it out of a concern to keep Sada from the temptations in these regions where people said the women had a reputation for fatal beauty? She'd been thrilled, certainly, to give herself the chance at the change of scenery she'd always dreamed of: green lands of water and lush foliage, between hills, streams, and mysteries. Dazzling million-colored flora. Practically a paradise on earth for a botanist like her.

Borso had dropped everything: the theater classes she was giving at the School of Fine Arts and the plays she put on in her courtyard, now transformed into a theater space, baptized the Empire of Illusion.

The adventure lasted two years, during which time they devoted themselves body and soul to Diéry. They had neither time nor desire—except on very rare occasions—to take long walks on chaotic trails, under the reddish dome of a thick fog. The cute and charming villa Sada had plunked down smack in the middle of a little paradise surrounded by hills offered the opportunity to quench any thirst for dreams, diversion, and discoveries.

Yacine figured she'd gotten in enough of her essential priority—the scientific benefits of this intoxicating experience—and had no trouble convincing Sada of the need to get back home.

Borso gets up and heads for the dining room.

Five minutes later, she's back with a tray.

The silence finally broken, Diéry gets up. He takes his father's hand in both of his.

"I'm sorry, Dad. I didn't want to make you angry." Warm response from Sada.

A shiver of emotion in everyone else. Joy, tenderness. A sense of deliverance.

"My boy, you didn't do anything wrong," says Boly. "It's actually Sada who crossed the line. Dear friend, it's not for having stuck the title His Excellency on Macoumba that we're reproaching you, but the fact that you showered him with praise."

The crowd is visibly intrigued.

"As a minister of the Republic, he certainly deserves that title."

"Oh, really?!"

"There's a bunch of numbskulls in that group, huh!" tosses out Yacine.

"Exactly!" confirms Mignane. "It's when we rush to stick it on the president of the Republic that it gets complicated."

"Say it straight out," shouts Borso. "It sure seems like you're trying to turn yourself into a lackey or—"

"Or just plain ignorance?" Mignane wonders. And he adds: "While actually degrading the president that way, according to some."

"Whoa!"

"Yes, objectively speaking. Like giving a general the title of colonel. Here, the Excellencies are the ambassadors. Words have weight."

"Right! Weigh and counterweigh the meaning of words."

"Uncle, what's the unit of measurement for weighing words?"

Bursts of laughter. Diéry waits for the answer, straight-faced.

"I'll tell you more about it next time, my boy. Now, I get the feeling that *ataya* is about to take precedence again."

Sada, Boly, Mignane: a wonderful story of fraternity and fidelity fed by the cordial values of honesty, dignity, courage, and perseverance inculcated by their parents. At a certain moment of their existence, the three of them lacked everything, or almost. Everything but the minimum to maintain their families with dignity and without complaints or lamentations.

Mignane's father was a driver for an agricultural company; Boly's, a farmer who fled his plot to switch to selling fruits and vegetables at the neighborhood market; Sada's, a mason who, after the collapse of a building under construction, decided to go into selling bric-a-brac on a street corner.

Luck had brought the three families together in a rental house. A populous neighborhood at the edge of the city. Three shacks without water or electricity. A hut in the corner of the courtyard for a toilet. A courtyard spacious enough for all the domestic activities: laundry, cooking, shooting the breeze, drumming, dancing and shows on occasion, play space for the kids. Good humor reigned there. They shared without any ulterior motives the jubilation and fervor of their respective religious holidays. Everyone in warm and cordial understanding.

In their hearts, they saw the bright side of everything. They all had the feeling of belonging to a family unit forged by blood ties.

Collective memory had doubtless engraved in the adults' minds the famous proverb they'd heard time and time again in their youth, in order to pass it on to their offspring: "*Nit nit ay garabam*, the human being is the remedy for humankind." Being neither deaf nor blind, much less idiots, they sorrowfully witnessed the degradation of the principles that gave meaning to that saying, seen as old-fashioned, lame, or dumb in certain people's eyes.

Their peace and quiet only lasted three years. Three years during which the drought had rudely tested the rural world and sparked a mass exodus toward the city. The return of the rainy season hit like a living hell for them and for the inhabitants of the other neighborhoods that had popped up like toadstools all across the city, without gutters or sewers. The house was summarily plopped in a basin, the rickety shacks pitching and swaying with the wind and rain in an enormous pool of nauseating sewage that carried along all sorts of filth.

Get out! That became an absolute necessity, if only to save the children. Sada must have been about six years old; Boly and Mignane, almost seven. Their parents insisted on registering them at the neighborhood school at the beginning of the next school year that was coming up. Not far from there, they found a solid house that wasn't flooded, but they gave up as early as the first few weeks. An infernal atmosphere polluted by the fights and squabbles among all the renters. The only reasonable solution was to return to their respective home regions: Boly and his parents to an island of mangroves and coconut palms; Mignane and his in the heart of a paradise on earth, shaded from the heat and also swept by the invigorating breath of the Ocean. Mapaté had decided to migrate to near the edge of a protected forest, in an area that housed a dump—now that everyone already called him *Boudjou*, or trash-picker, because of his bric-a-brac.

For a long time, he'd shouted his indignation when young and old pinned that disparaging nickname on him: "I'm not *Boudjou*! My name is Mapaté Waar, son of Beug Deug Waar and Bagne Gathié Ndiaye. Everyone from Saloum knows them."

People laughed in his face and continued calmly on their way. "A *boudjou*, a trash-picker, who dares to claim his right to respect! *Hiii! Kii, sagarou nit rek la*, that guy is a rag of a man," one passerby had dared say.

That day, *Boudjou* (sorry, Mapaté) had thrashed the impertinent man. Mapaté's leg broken, but his honor intact. A crowd, salacious insults, the police because the victim was in a pitiable state with a black eye and a bloody mouth. An incredibly gentle police officer had said to Mapaté, "Big guy, you shouldn't pay any more attention to what these worthless people say!"

Mapaté's salt-of-the-earth wife, Sabou, backed up the police officer. "I always tell him that. We have to understand that there's no more *yermandé*, no more humanity . . . no more good upbringing."

Like a true pragmatic intelligent *Saloum-Saloum*, *Boudjou* understood the advice. What good is it to waste his spit and nerves on brainless creatures?!

Mapaté began to work his "field."[2] That's how he talked about the dump. A way, in his heart, to evoke his generous home turf, his village, his community. Above all, to live this time together, in perfect communion and in permanent dialogue, with all the mysterious whispers and shadows and beings that make up the invisible but absolutely real "peoples" of the earth, the sky, the water, the plants.

---

2. This is a reference to the phrase, *Yalla Yalla Bey sa toll*, which in its literal sense means, "Call to God all you want, but work your own field first." Sabou uses the phrase later in the novel.

Ignore the stinking rivulets, the mass of dust and black smoke above everyone's head. "A man worthy of that name has to conquer difficulties without shameful, sterile laments," he loved to repeat to Sada when he was just a little kid.

But he couldn't help sometimes remembering the warnings recently put forth by Mignane's father: "The place is magnificent. Between the forest, the Ocean, and the rivers. It's incredible how people are spoiling it right before our eyes. Hundreds of hectares handed over to industrialists who really know how to earn money. Can we blame them? Except that the local workers don't collect anything but crumbs, and they make do because all anyone worries about is protecting their own interests."

"*Dooley daan*," replied Mapaté, smiling—might makes right.

"*Dooley daan*, it's true. But you've got to believe in it, and want it! When I go back to my region, I'll work my land with my family. We can do as much as those people who are exploiting our lands. We've got to convince ourselves that we can!"

"You're still brawny!" scoffed Mapaté, his kola-reddened teeth all showing. Then, more seriously: "If bric-a-brac allows me to support my little family, to bring the kids up right, I'll already have earned my paradise on earth, and even in the afterlife, because I'll have accomplished my duty of taking care of my family and sharing as much as possible the little I've earned."

"You should also know that it's not unusual for criminals hiding in the forest to show up."

"We'll see about that," Mapaté cut in. "What good would it do them to attack a man who's aged before his time . . . infirm . . . indigent?"

"Indigent?! No! Don't say that again," said Mignane's father. "Listen, Mapaté, my grandfather taught me *Nit day nitté*: a human being must carry the values that honor his condition—that is to say, true human riches—by his dignity, the ineffable dimension of his personality. That dimension that, by sense and reason, animates his soul, his heart, his consciousness. And that inspires in him a sense of duty—or, better, the reflex of safeguarding the honorability of his condition."

"It's true. It's true that I was wrong to project onto myself the opinion of people who no longer respect anyone or anything. In truth, I can't complain."

Listening to the two men, Sabou had felt a pinch of bitterness. Apt to pick up on Mapaté's slightest hints, she'd sensed a sort of lassitude in her husband since that awful insult, "*Sagarou nit,* rag-man!" He would never forget. And would never say it. She'd known him immune to discouragement and moral discomfort in the face of the most difficult situations. "Of course," she said to herself, "in this world where hearts seem to have dried out, where no one loves or misses anything anymore, where we hurt those close to us with no remorse, you need nerves of steel." And she'd decided never to let him falter.

After a long silence, Mapaté had picked up the thread again. Addressing Mignane's father: "It's true that times have changed."

"You're right. Times, morals, habits have all changed. It's inevitable—let's just hope the fundamental human capital comes out of it okay. Let's just hope it doesn't perish."

Sada had been there for that conversation. True that it had weighed heavily on his heart to separate from Boly and Mignane. True also that children love adventure and worry little about the risks. Very young—six? seven?—he had a vivacity of body and spirit that impressed everyone who saw him. Moving, running, jumping: "Like a *niébé*[3] seed in a boiling pot," his sweet mother Sabou would repeat, a smile on her lips. *Tioprane!*[4] she would shout, while savoring in her heart the boy's moving readiness to be of service to others, at home and in the

3. "Bean."
4. "Turbulent."

neighborhood: running errands, politely declining the coins or treats that people wanted to offer him in return, in accordance with his parents' strict orders; carrying on his frail shoulders a load grabbed from the hands of out-of-breath adults; participating in housework—all to his parents' great joy.

Adorable kid. Even his joyful pranks, however surprising they might be, enchanted the adults. Like capturing lizards in a basket and letting them loose in a gathering of chatting adults, sowing panic and collecting oaths that very quickly blew away in the wind. Everything would end in laughs.

At the "dump," he pretty quickly got used to his favorite game: imitating birdsongs. Responding to them and feeling intoxicated to be participating in this sublime dawn concert, before reciting his Qur'an lesson to his teacher, who was none other than his father: Mapaté Waar. Then, ready to savor a bowl of millet porridge accented by a layer of palm oil. Millet porridge: the magic, the perfume of that *souna*, that minuscule olive-green grain of millet, under its blanket of buttermilk and the warm film of palm oil! Such a treat: "Oh what a delicacy!" Then, finally ready to collect deadwood for the kitchen for Sabou, who would already be on her way to the public spigot in the next neighborhood over, accompanied by her two daughters: Dior, six months old, arms bouncing, legs dangling; and Siga, four years old, proudly holding on to a miniature bucket. She would collect affectionate teasing—"*Ey*, Crybaby, don't think you can fool me, your pail is leaky, for sure!"—but also tons of packets of peanuts, fritters, and other treats from the vendors around the spigot.

Only deadwood. Sada wouldn't touch the branches or even the twigs that were visibly dry and only waiting for a breeze to come off and land on the dirt.

Our story is made of history: right away, the day after the first night spent at "the dump," under the tight-laid leaves of the eucalyptus trees, the tufted branches of the centenary baobabs and giant acacias, a sudden reminiscence had brought Sada back to the territory of his youth that he left when he wasn't even three years old.

Above their heads, Mapaté busied himself finishing the task he'd undertaken the night before: attaching around solid trunks the straw mats that were to serve as a roof for the summarily laid-out shack, to shelter the family.

In the fog of dawn, the way several colonies of birds would take off and send the foliage shaking in all directions fascinated Sada. His childhood passion emerged like a miracle. He had peeked between the branches and felt a deep jubilation: the multitude of nests, their diversity, the impressive size of some of them, the incredible weaving! Enough to make anyone marvel. And to wonder out loud that the birds were able to do as much as—maybe more than—his uncle Birane, Sabou's brother whom Sada hadn't met. Birane: an unequaled cane weaver whose reputation had traveled beyond the boundaries of the region. All that's left of him is the legend Sabou often brings up: "*Tiey*, Birane! It made you dizzy to watch his fingers crisscross like a machine around the long vines that hung about his face. *Tiey*, Birane! The most surprising thing was that he kept his eyes closed while the work slid gracefully between his fingers. When out of that he pulled bins, mats, baskets, you really felt like an invisible force was inspiring him."

Silence.

And then Sabou would wipe away the tears that welled up and fell on her beautiful face. And she'd continue with a heavy heart: "The devil, *Seytani*, took him off in those unhappy boatloads! Birane could live on the fruit of his labor, which guaranteed him peace and security. Will he come back someday? God is great! *Seytani* made him lose his way."

"Wrong," Mapaté cut in. "*Seytani* is us, ourselves: our greed, our outsized desires, our taste for convenience. *Liguey dieurignou*, living off one's work. To harvest, you need to plant, to wait, to persevere in the effort. We don't say it to the youth anymore. Parents no longer have the time to take on the sacred duty of raising their kids well; they even encourage them to sacrifice their lives for hypothetical riches."

Silence.

Sada, busy making a miniature bicycle out of metal wire. Tinkering is his passion.

Sabou again, her voice low, really talking to herself: "Birane surprised everyone. He was generous, humble, reasonable."

"No doubt," responded Mapaté sweetly. "Maybe well educated too. The most difficult thing is to resist the siren call of illusions."

Silence.

Then Mapaté again, in his serene voice, the one of mumbled *zikrs*, moving solitary litanies that greet the first glimmers of the emerging sun: "Sada, did you hear what I just said?"

"Yes, Father, I heard it fine."

"You heard. How?"

"Not just with my ears. In my head, in my heart, in my veins." Smiling as if to tease his father and show him that he'd truly assimilated the stock phrase.

With Mapaté, each day brought its own lesson. A story to tell, a fable, a memory either playful or serious. Once in a while, a little play in the shade of a majestic tamarind tree just across from the shack. A jaunty Mapaté played the main role while Sabou sang with her nightingale's voice and took care of the rhythm, beating the back of a gourd for a drum. The "dump" regulars and the people across the way, on the market side, came running to add their part, to the great joy of everyone, Sada in particular. "Entertainment is part of life; it gives the heart a big breath of fresh air," concluded Mapaté.

Constantly, at his very core, he was always keeping an eye out for the well-being of the "immense richness"—as he put it—that he'd accumulated over time. Not in gold, not in little sacks stuffed with silver at the bottom of a case, not in notoriety. But the joy of living in balance, in himself and alongside others in order to conquer the traps of life.

Education and good upbringing, naturally. But also the quest for "life experience." Mapaté had taught Sada that for a young man, that was a crucial step in his physical, moral, and spiritual development. "One day," he'd said, "you'll be sent out on the hazardous path of adventure. When you're able to dissect the lessons and precepts of the Qur'an, you'll be allowed to 'go forth' toward other horizons to deepen your knowledge, not necessarily related to religious questions. Almost a rite-of-passage trip into the labyrinth of life and the complexity of the world."

Sada was thrilled.

Later, much later, when he would announce to his father that he'd found a young woman he wanted to marry, Mapaté would feel a strong emotion. As if his grandfather Serigne Modou Waar had come back to life. The image of the great man would burst forth. Just as he'd always seen him, dressed in his mantle of humility and wisdom. This mysterious present flitting through at the speed of a shooting star would seem like a good omen to him. Serigne Modou Waar, a legend.

Mapaté never tired of telling Sada: "I thank God and my grandfather for taking me into his *daara*, open-air school, in the bush, far from the houses—oh, a few huts, nothing exciting. But human warmth in every season. Lots of students at the Qur'anic school, *ndongos* come from every corner of the region, from modest or comfortable backgrounds, but all subject to the same discipline: fieldwork to make sure there was food and rigorous studying.

"One day, my grandfather called me into his room. Books everywhere and tons of manuscripts written in his hand. As usual, he was seated on layered sheepskins. Above his head, the only window in the room distilled the dull light of the last rays of the setting sun. He smiled and said to me, a bit teasingly: 'Mapaté, you are at present a man in the fullness of your strength, may God be praised! It's come to my attention that you outclass the boys of your generation in the ring and that all the girls in the land would like to marry you.'

"'I'll be sure not to be your rival. I'd never get out of that unscathed,' I replied. The classic joke brought laughs all around. Little girls played the 'rivals' of their grandmothers; the little boys, of their grandfathers.

"More seriously, he continued: 'Mapaté, I think that you can leave the *daara*. You know the tradition. Write me a little text. A beautiful text, in our language written in Arabic script, like these'—pointing to a pile of pages meticulously arranged on a trunk—'about love, preferably about women. Where there isn't love, *yermandé* won't prosper. Or about the forces of nature: earth, water, air, and fire. Show how you have understood what is said about them throughout the precepts you've learned in the Book.'

"Naturally, I'd chosen to prepare a text about love. Love and the woman. Woman! In herself, the nourishing earth from which sprouts the seeds that populate the universe. In herself, the air that aerates and excites our senses for better and, also, for worse. In herself, the fire that illuminates our lives just as it can consume our heart . . . and ruin our existence! It all depends."

That phrase was left hanging, falling through the silence. Then Mapaté continued: "I concluded that in all things, I'd adopt the motto 'for better or worse.' But for the one I'd hoped to marry"—smiling without naming Sabou—"I'd only hoped for the better. I delivered the text two days later; at the time, he'd told me: 'When the sun is at its zenith. In Arabic script, in our language.' The next day, in the early morning, he called me in. 'Mapaté! May God bless your path. Come back to us more solid, stronger, the head full. And don't forget where you come from.'"

Mapaté knew that this stock phrase would come in handy one day. He'd understood that well, like the majority of those who'd left and returned unscathed after having seen and learned a lot. "Where you come from" didn't suggest any reference to origins, belongings, social status, or religious affiliation. It called up the fundamental principles methodically tested, forged, and transmitted in order to fashion human beings with respect for the cardinal values that guarantee *diom*, dignity and honor. On the immovable pedestal of love, tolerance, generosity, and justice. And above all: humility.

No one had ever heard Mapaté brag about being the grandson of Serigne Modou Waar, eminent scholar, descendant of a prestigious lineage of the Mandingue empire, since shattered into thousands of pieces by the whims of endless wars and the colonial invasion.

One day, at "the dump," the horizon darkened, shaking up all of a sudden the routine of an existence that was quite serene, when all is said and done. A morning of fog thickened by truck fumes. A biting cold that reached all the way down to the deepest spot.

Under a pile of rubble, doing his daily "harvest" in the garbage, Mapaté had spotted a bit of a sleeve. Jacket? Blazer? He'd pulled with all his might to extract it from both the rubble and a sticky substance that wouldn't let go. Mapaté wore himself out, his fingers frozen. He pulled, pulled, worked away.

The mass eventually came loose. A big ball from which emerged a long pleather sleeve. An ageless, colorless jacket.

While he kept trying to get it back in shape, four big youths came out of the woods. One of them came up to Mapaté. A nasty look, a sharp tone, a rough voice. He ordered, "Put that back where you found it!"

Mapaté clearly didn't understand at all. In a flash, the man's fist crushed down like a bomb on his face. Mapaté fell. The man snickered like a satisfied ogre seeing him slumped so sadly. One of his three other companions sent a well-aimed kick to Mapaté's backside as he tried to get up. Not the slightest sigh. Mapaté didn't interrupt his effort to get up.

Supreme humiliation! Sabou had seen the whole scene from the corner where she was grinding the millet for her couscous. She showed up without a sound where this brutality was staged: huge strides, mute face, enigmatic. She was holding one knob of her pestle in her right hand. She came forward swinging.

Sabou! Where no one would have expected her! Surprising everyone, in a few seconds she'd raised the pestle with both hands high above her head. She aimed for the hoodlum's head, she hit . . . Sabou! Herself! Little bit of a woman as graceful as a doe.

Sabou hit. No one had ever seen her fight or heard so much as an insult come out of her mouth. Sabou hit. To punish the wild beast.

Even the undesirable guests were surprised. Dumbstruck! Stupefied!

One of the aggressor's companions, stiff as a pike up until that point, opportunely grabbed the pestle with quickness and agility. A master stroke! In his line of work, for sure. He helped Mapaté stand up. A minute of glacial silence. Then, in a voice dripping with tenderness, his hand on Sabou's shoulder, he said: "Sorry, Mother. This will never happen again.

Those guys who attacked the old man are new. This will never happen again."

He gave a stern look to the attacker, who seemed like he was hypnotized. The three louts "skedaddled," having doubtless understood their companion's unstated message. That companion took the pestle. He walked with Mapaté and Sabou to the door of their shack. The little girls were still fast asleep inside.

It was at that moment that Sada arrived, a bundle of wood on his head, another under his arm. He would never know anything at all of what had just happened. "No need to tell him," whispered Mapaté when the "fourth man" had turned tail after promising to return. "Sparking hate in a child's heart—what good would that do?"

"It's true," replied Sabou. "Hate is a poison. Later, when Sada is stronger in his head, we will tell him, God willing. That's also life. This stupid, sad affair is part of his life and of ours. He'll be mature and responsible enough to laugh about it."

"You think? Everything can be laughed at except humiliation. In the best case, he'll suffer from it."

"It's true, Mapaté. You talk like a saint."

"I'm far from being one, for sure! But I've learned that peace in the heart and in the soul is worth any and all sacrifice. One of the lessons I got from my grandfather! *Tiey*, Serigne Modou Waar! An endangered species. For sure!"

Everyone drinks from the wellspring of a cultural heritage hidden since the beginning of time in the bowels of the earth. Did Sabou know the epic of those valiant heroines who, one way or another, in times of peace, war, or catastrophe, wrote the most beautiful lines in Humanity's story? The big story, which we sometimes call "history," and the small personal story—which is not of a lower order. Those heroines, with their bravura, their knowledge, their know-how, their patience—which is neither passivity nor indifference. With their serenity, which is not weakness, but a prodigious mental power.

Did Sabou know at least a bit of it? Maybe yes, maybe no. Some say that a woman's belly is an ocean: immense, unfathomable, mysterious.

She knew the song, at least. A delicious melody that, for all of eternity, had managed to follow the paths of the winds, to make its way into the cottages and stick: *Bagne gathia, nangou dé*, death before dishonor.

That was in the time when dishonor was fatal.

As promised, the "fourth man"—as Mapaté called him—came back the next day to hear the family's news. The face of an angel.

"How could this young man have played around with those troublemakers who've infested the forest?" Mapaté and Sabou asked themselves so many times.

As the days went by, they got used to his almost-daily visits, keeping a discreet eye on his conversations with Sada. Those talks were exclusively about birds, the wildlife in the fields, monkeys, squirrels, rats, turtles. Fascinating discoveries sharpened Sada's curiosity. In the long run, they heard nothing worrisome that could inspire mistrust. Even still, the principle of precaution didn't prevent Sabou from asking the questions that were bugging her.

"Sada calls you Bougouma;[5] is that really your name?"

"Yes, Mother."

"D'you live in the facing neighborhood or in the forest?"

"No. Actually, I don't live anywhere."

"*Hii!* My son! What's that? You don't live anywhere?" adding, "Well, your family, then?"

---

5. "He whom no one wants anything to do with" in Wolof.

Bougouma's face tensed up. That detail didn't escape Sabou. Nevertheless, she kept up her questioning, but gently.

"*Dome!*[6] In the village? In the city? Like us: from the village to the city? It was nice to live out there in the village. We never know how to appreciate what God's given us. In the city, we were in hell in the heart of the big city."

"Me? Nothing, nowhere. I've always been shunted around from place to place in a big black hole. I'm trying to find my way. Since I met you all, I have the feeling for the first time in my life . . . to glimpse a little ray of light."

"How old are you?"

"I don't know. During the elections, politicians 'scooped up' here and there thousands of young people like me; they made us make up ID cards and voter registration cards. They declared I was twenty years old. I must have been less than sixteen. There were a bunch of others who didn't look like they could have been more than fourteen. Ten, even. They paid a thousand francs per card to the middleman, took all the cards . . . and left. Nowadays, people tell me I don't look more than twenty. The people that 'scooped us up' in the markets or on street corners, and certain 'bosses,' confiscated the money and threatened us with prison if we denounced them."

"Mapaté and I have never voted. Good for us."

"Now I might be eighteen . . . or twenty! That's my reality. I'm from nowhere. I go around and around, come to 'the dump' sometimes to find things here and there, whatever I can find to sell in addition to my job as a porter in the market across the way."

Silence. Then: "Those three big guys you saw have been hanging out on the other side of the hill for some time now. It's just dumb luck that we found ourselves here that day. We'd already

6. "My son" in Wolof.

had some rough fights, during which my friends and I got the upper hand. They respect me. Here, it's the law of the jungle. The strongest is respected."

All of a sudden, it was as if he got a bone stuck in his throat. He broke down in tears, got up, headed toward the sea on the other side of one of the hills that border the forest. A few meters away, he turned around. His hand up high, he waved an empty jute sack. Sada understood and also got his own sack and ran to join him.

The two of them at the beach to finish the chore of shoring up around the family's shack. The white sand sparkling under the sun, big boulders around the edges, to give Sabou a spacious courtyard and Mapaté a space to rest when he'd finished carrying out his work. And also—most importantly, perhaps—a convivial place for *waxtaan*, that salutary shooting the breeze, and all the other leisure activities that, according to Mapaté, "air out the heart and the soul." The place would draw everyone there. Not just anyone. "Good company," who would know how to talk, how to have fun, how to respect each other outside of any divisions, be they social, ethnic, or religious.

In fact, right from the day of that incident no one will speak of again, Bougouma had felt a magnetic force coming from Sabou that lit up her face, sang in her voice, and directed her gestures. Even on that day when, but for his own quickness, she would have committed a very serious act that would have landed her in prison.

That day there had sprung up in his heart, for the very first time in his life, that spark: warm, uncontrollable, magic. That instinct of love directed toward another. For the first time, he heard in his heart the delightful call of parent-child tenderness. In Sabou, he found that day a mother: generous, sweet, intransigent too. A miracle.

He would never, never, absolutely never ever—for fear of showing his wounds—tell of the cruelty he'd endured. Slavery in its hardest, most abject, most dishonoring forms, sometimes in the clutches of adults above all suspicion but rotted by vice and brutality.

When a group of teenagers carried him off at knifepoint one early morning from the corner where he was begging, he was afraid, of course (a normal reflex). But he told himself that after all he couldn't really imagine anything worse than the cruelties he'd already endured. They dragged him into their racket in one of the busiest markets in the city, and of course, into the need to fight in order to get by. He'd become a pro at unlocking cars so quickly that the head of his gang nicknamed him "Automatic." Arrested and sent to prison for a year for having stolen a laptop and a cell phone from a well-secured luxury car, he'd been freed thanks to the goodwill of some prison guards who had sensed that he could be reformed. They gave him advice on how he could earn a living by turning his hustle into something legal. He swore in tears that he would.

Bougouma ended up gaining everyone's trust. Now a full-fledged member of the family, he benefited wholeheartedly from Sabou and Mapaté's caring attention—the same as they showed to their own children—without being spared from following the household's operating code of conduct: principles of a rigorous upbringing, intelligently instilled, without insults or teasing.

Bougouma took to that code with enthusiasm. Aware of having lost a lot of time in understanding the point of his own existence. Up until that point, he'd been tossed around by the destructive waves and surges of a cruel world.

He savored the incredible luck of "having finally found parents, a brother, and two sisters." That's how he felt it in his sunlit heart. Sometimes even monologuing to himself in the middle of the night in the little room he'd ended up renting nearby.

He taught Sada to make fishing nets. With such dexterity that suddenly one day, Sabou had shed a tear watching him. She thought of her Birane, sadly carried off by the perilous adventure of the one-way pirogues.

Sada and Bougouma decided to take up fishing. On the other side of the hill next to "the dump," a big lake spread out its iridescent splendor, which was seriously degraded by floating garbage and all sorts of detritus.

Giving, giving . . . instinctively. Bougouma lent an expert hand to Sada to allow him to refine the gadgets fashioned out of all the little loose scraps picked up at the blacksmiths' shops. What pride, to know himself capable of creating with his own hands these complex objects that his parents enjoyed! Not to mention the immense joy of giving them to his sisters. And to feel, on seeing their amazed faces, how thrilled they were to be able to enrich their lineup of toys, which up until then had consisted of beautiful dolls artistically crafted by Sabou with clothes and accessories made from scraps of cloth picked up at the tailor's.

For his part, even though he was so much younger, Sada helped Bougouma polish his language, simply by putting Mapaté's "lessons" to the melody of a little song and laughing: "Don't insult people, *waay waay* / no swear words, *waay waay* / even in hard times, even in hard times, *waay waay* / which doesn't keep you from being respected, *waay waay*."

"*Waané wa!* Little wise guy!" replied Bougouma, laughing. Then, seriously: "Thank you, little brother, all the same. I'm the one who should have been correcting you. But watch out! Don't get cocky. All honor is due to our parents. You were just lucky enough to learn before me." Then, all-out playful teasing.

The fishing proved fruitful. Sabou got first dibs, according to her preferences each day. She loved *dèmes* (freshwater mullets) and trout. All the rest went right into housewives' baskets or the fishmongers' crates to be sold fresh or dried.

The bicycles, *cars rapides*, and other miniature gadgets grew in scale, caliber, precision, and enticing colors. Traveling merchants bought them on the spot, under the tamarind tree baptized henceforth as "the Waars' Tamarind" by the regulars at the neighborhood's much-loved "break times." The merchants then resold them at the downtown craft market, where tourists ate them up. Little by little, the burden of sorting through the trash was consigned to the memory shelf. Except that Mapaté refused to sit back and do nothing. He still went there from time to time, often just to look out at the horizon. The simple pleasure of moving. "Immobility doesn't work for me!" And he'd burst out laughing.

Their reflex, right from the first accounting of two years' activity: give their profit to Mapaté, who, just like Sabou, hadn't shown any curiosity about their earnings, being already satisfied with the boys' contribution to lightening the daily expenses.

"Elegant gesture," Mapaté had said soberly. He'd taken the money in his hands an instant before adding, "What a great pride to see our children work and earn a salary with the sweat of their brow. I will take this"—a 5,000-franc bill*—"The same for your mother"—giving the bill to Sabou. He gave the rest back to them without counting it. "Keep this money. Spend it wisely. The future is waiting for you. Still, some advice: memory is not a faithful friend. Get a notebook and write down your spending and your income."

With a confused expression, they looked at him. Then, Sada: "Father, you do it! We don't know how to write."

---

* Translator's note: A little less than ten US dollars.

Mapaté's burst of laughter. Then: "What did you do this very morning when you put a surah on Bougouma's tablet?"

Sada, confused: "But that's his lesson for the day!"

"How'd you get it onto the tablet?"

"With the *xalima* and the *dâ*, pen and ink."

"And that's not writing? To manage my bric-a-brac business, I always put everything down in my notebook." And he took a notebook out from a trunk and spread out before their eyes columns, numbers, and letters. "Tell me, Sada, you really can't read and write?"

"Well, yes, Father! This stuff, I know. Really, I meant that I can't do it in—"

"I know what you mean." Laughter. Then: "What you know how to do, you can do in a thousand languages! If you have the opportunity. My grandfather spoke five languages and wrote Arabic and Swahili! You can widen your horizon to other languages."

"At school—"

"There are as many schools as there are languages!"

"You're right, Father. I'm thinking of the *toubabs'* school."

"Why not, if you can!"

"I dream of that!" exclaimed Sada. "I'll get to it as soon as I can."

"Me too!" said Bougouma.

"*InshAllah*," concluded Mapaté. "May God bless your intention. It's never too late to learn. My grandfather repeated that constantly."

Really, Bougouma and Sada knew a thing or two about small business. They'd taken turns running the bric-a-brac table when Mapaté left for the village as the traditional holidays were approaching.

Visiting family to maintain the connection. Contributing, as much as his savings would permit, to the family's supplies. And feeling enlivened, breathing deep into his lungs the soothing breeze of concord.

A few days later, Sada brought the subject up again. "Father, can I really go to school?"

"If God wishes it, sure you can . . . at your age. It's never too late, I tell you again."

Giddy joy in Sada's heart. Just then, an image popped up, a miraculous unexpected memory: Boly and Mignane, the day they parted ways, in the house of shacks floating on a layer of greenish stinking water. That was a long time ago. He hadn't noticed the years fly by. Boly and Mignane! A future in school had been open to them by the hazards of fortune. He hadn't even considered it for himself. No acting out or jealousy, though. Not the least frustration that day. Believing perhaps that the luxury of going to the *toubab* school wasn't written in his destiny as a descendant of Serigne Modou Waar, a villager who was cloistered day and night in his room when he'd finished at dawn his work in the fields and hurried to regain his world: his hut on a little laterite hill, his stacked-up sheepskins that served as prayer rug and reading spot; his library: a wooden trunk with a goatskin cover that used to shine but was crackled with age.

Sada still hadn't learned any of the fabulous story of his great-grandfather, whose legend was fading away slowly into the waves of desert sand. He didn't know that his great-grandfather Serigne Modou Waar had traveled by foot, donkey, camel, and then some! On old tubs across deserts, streams, lakes, and rivers. At the whim of the wind and the seasons, he'd been mason, driver, docker.

Without ever tiring of assiduously frequenting mosques and madrassas in whose courtyards he would spend the night, if

not on the quays or—supreme happiness!—on the edge of the
caravans, among the little businesses that pop up at their every
stop. The fair-like ambiance, colors and voices: the hawkers'
concert. The camels fascinated him! He'd grab every chance
to serve as camel steward to the great satisfaction of the camel
herders won over by his courtesy, his passion while working,
the respect he immediately inspired, and his humility.

At twenty-five, figuring he'd properly accomplished the mission that his father, Birima, gave him—to discover the world
and never forget where he came from—Serigne Modou Waar
headed back home. He had seen and learned, and he knew that
the adventure didn't end there.

One morning, at dawn, a cart dropped him off at his childhood home with his case full of papers onto which he'd copied
texts from ancient manuscripts picked up here and there: religious texts, secular poems. And also: copies of engravings and
drawings of venerated places and symbols.

"Serigne Modou Waar! *Gathié Ngallama!* The family honor
is safe!" his father had said.

The very next day, a glorious party was held in his honor. The
village and the whole surrounding area had sung in chorus:
"*Diarrama,*[7] Modou Waar! *Gathié Ngallama!*"

It was while trying to follow in the footsteps of his illustrious
grandfather that Mapaté fractured his leg falling from the top
of a crumbling building in a neighborhood of a prosperous city
in the east of the continent.

One day, Sada and Bougouma surprised Mapaté. Sada, grin-
ning from ear to ear: "Father, from this day forward, you are
finished with 'the dump.' 'The table,' too. That's now a business
for us two"—pointing to Bougouma.

7. "Thank you."

"What do you mean?! I need to work, to move! To put in my sweat equity to survive!" Mapaté said again with energy. "I'm telling you again."

"You'll move around, Father." And Bougouma, the "elder," went rattling three keys on a cord. The two of them put the cord around his neck.

"You now have a store at the market, at the corner of the big road. A small shop, for sure . . . but your bric-a-brac will fit in there and even other popular products and food supplies. Little by little, you'll have to look after it, of course. And us too."

Sabou let out a spontaneous cry of joy and started reciting prayers. "May God bless you!"

Mapaté was overcome by emotion. His eyes welled up, and he hurried, as if he were embarrassed, to wipe his face with the edge of his caftan sleeve. Sabou's heart tingled and sent a sparkling flash over her face. Addressing Mapaté, she said, "It is desirable for any parent to cry with joy when our children do more than we could have hoped for. These tears that you're hiding (while laughing) are a blessing. May God spare us the horrible misfortune to cry over our offspring's depravity."

Sada felt in that moment like he'd taken a huge stride on the path of his dreams. He would "become" Serigne Modou Waar, that erudite man respected beyond the boundaries of that tiny village lost in the savanna sands. He would "become . . ." He would have his adventure, just like Serigne Modou Waar had had his. Differently, of course. He would "head out" to discover the world. He would go to school.

Sada and Bougouma have finished working out the particulars of managing all the affairs they had going: fishing, household chores, taking turns at the store to keep Mapaté company. The neighborhood isn't safe. It's Bougouma, the "eldest," who stands guard.

Sada has made the decision to bluff his way into school. He takes the Filao tree-lined path: five or six hundred meters to get to the school, the only public establishment in this overpopulated zone. It's exactly seven a.m. when he crosses the threshold of the dilapidated building. He knows that classes start at eight. He greets the snack sellers busy stocking their stalls and makes a beeline for the director's office, having located it during a reconnaissance visit the night before. He doesn't hold back from taking a peek inside since the door is ajar.

A cleaning woman shows up.

"Hello, Mother."

Huge and agreeable surprise on the young lady's part. She is comforted, for this natural gesture of greeting people one doesn't know has become so rare.

"You want to see the director?"

"Yes, Mother. I would like to see him."

"He won't be here until after the bell rings. When everyone's in class."

"Thank you, Mother. I'll wait."

The cleaning woman pushes with her ratty broom the thick layer of sand that's built up on the cement slab. Once at his level, she asks him to go over to the other end of the veranda.

The courtyard fills up progressively. It's swarming all around like at a fair. Later, a strident bell. Rows are formed. The courtyard empties. Sada's heart beats a little faster. But he stays calm.

A man arrives. Runs his disdainful gaze over Sada from head to toe. He goes into the office, comes right back out. Sada tells himself that this slovenly man surely isn't the director.

But . . . who knows? He greets him despite it all.

"Hello, Father."

"Hello. What do you want?"

"To see the director."

"Was he there when you got here?"

"It seems he doesn't come to his office until after making sure all the students have gotten into class."

"Of course!" he scoffed. "That's obvious."

Sada asked himself why the guy bothered to ask him that if it was so obvious.

"Do you have an appointment?"

"No, Father."

"You know him? Family connections?"

"I've never met him. I would simply like to see him today."

"To get hired . . . or helped out of a jam . . . in these hard times?"

"No, Father. I've come to sign up for school."

The man almost suffocated. Huge mocking laugh. Then: "You, a big guy your age. Are you joking? This is a primary school!"

A little smile from Sada. Still—always—Zen.

The director showed up right at the moment when the man was choking down his own venomous spit.

"Hello, Mor."

"Hi, Mbengue."

"Hello, young man."

"Hello, Uncle."

The director went into his office. Mor followed him, then came back out when the director had slipped him a 500-franc bill as usual, preceding him with tact toward the exit.

"You can come in, young man. Sit down."

Face-to-face with the director, Sada is moved. Proud of his audacity, he runs his gaze over the four corners of the room. Three walls covered floor to ceiling with shelves. Books, paintings, photographs, globes, all meticulously arranged. Also, piles of manuals and documents stacked up everywhere.

"My name is Baye Mbengue. And you?"

"My name is Sada Waar."

"Do you live around here?"

"In Les Filaos, not far."

"What have you done up until now?"

"Learning the Qur'an, fishing, making stuff, gardening. Recently, my big brother and I opened a little store for our parents, near the Filao tree market."

"Not bad, all that! Well, bravo!" exclaimed the director with childlike enthusiasm. "How old are you?"

"Eighteen. Well, actually, I don't know: a little more . . . or less," he added, reassured by the director's cheerfulness and simplicity.

"What made you want to sign up for school now?"

"To study. Really! And to go farther!"

"To earn a lot of money?"

Sada smiled. "Not only that, Uncle! Money is useful. But above all: to prove to myself that I can go farther with my abilities and my will to succeed."

The director, his twinkling eye on Sada. Sada, his eyes locked on the director's, with total confidence and serenity. "Well then! Let's see what we can do. I'm not a psychic, but I have a feeling that you'll succeed if you continue on your trajectory."

"*InshAllah! Amine*, Uncle."

The director stretched out his long form. A few steps toward a shelf. He pulled out a brochure. Flipping through it and coming back to his seat: "You know how to read and write Arabic, isn't that so?"

"Yes, I've gotten through the Qur'an seven times. I don't speak Arabic fluently, but I can translate the Qur'an into Wolof and Mandingue."

"Well now, that's not bad! Who taught you?"

"My father, Mapaté Waar."

The director, with a hint of nostalgia: "It was also my father who taught me. He was the head of the local Qur'anic school.

Before I started going to the French school at the age of nine. Take this French-Arabic syllabary. You can learn the French alphabet, plus a little vocabulary. The way I see you, this could go quite quickly. Come back in two months. I'll decide on which class to put you in, depending on your results . . . at the back of the class. You seem like a grounded, well-brought-up boy. You need that—along with will, effort, and discipline—to succeed."

"Thank you, my father! From the bottom of my heart."

"One piece of advice, all the same: don't pay any attention to nasty people's jibes, like 'ugly duckling' or 'camel in a herd of sheep'"—without specifically naming Mor. "It could come from kids or from stupid and bitter adults. Childhood is innocent . . . and it can also be cruel . . . without meaning to be."

"I know, Uncle. No problem. Thank you so much. *Dieureudieuf*,[8] Uncle."

The director walked him to the door. Proud and thrilled to have a chance to don once again his "savior" cloak. His friends and colleagues had affectionately pinned this nickname on him long ago, ever since, over the course of his multiple assignments across cities, villages, hamlets, forests, and savannas, he gave himself the mission of "fishing out" kids who were deaf, mute, blind, or in poverty. All condemned never to emerge from the shadows of ignorance. All because of their physical handicap or the resignation, destitution, or fatalism of their parents.

Two years later, Sada got his primary school certificate as an external candidate under the enlightened direction of his providential tutor. The director, alias Uncle Mbengue, had taken care to sign both Sada and Bougouma up in the civil register. Bougouma wanted to be officially registered under the identity of Taaw Waar, son of Mapaté Waar and Sabou Touré. As it was, for a while already no one in the house or the neighborhood had

---

8. "Thank you" in Wolof.

used anything but the first name *Taaw*, "the Eldest," a much more respectful name than *Bougouma*. Out of respect and affection. And, doubtless, to bury once and for all any reference to his prior misfortunes.

Tempted at first, Taaw ended up deciding not to accompany Sada on the school track.

"I feel good here," he'd explained. "Fishing, the store. Business is going well. I've chosen to take care of that, in the family's name. In these days, who can you trust? I want to go far, always farther, to succeed. Sada will do the same, in his way. Go for it, little brother!"—with a wide smile and a tap on Sada's shoulder.

"You're just dropping me like that?!" Sada had said with a teasing voice.

A concert of laughter.

Mapaté had responded gently, his heart filled with joy: "Each of you choose your path. May it not plunge you into chaos. The main thing is that you never, ever forget where you come from."

They understood, having heard this refrain so many times.

"May God protect you!"

"*Amine!*" from all the voices mixed together. Sabou in heaven.

Sada's success was considered an exceptional event in this area where the residents were mostly resigned to the idea that they were condemned to live forever in the mental, congenital, inexorable indigence they'd been hit with.

Uncle Mbengue took advantage of this "event" to convince them that success is acquired through effort and confidence in one's own abilities. In the packed school courtyard, he hammered: "Those who want to make us believe that poverty is our turf and there's no way out are a new breed of charlatan. They stuff themselves on the distress of the poor. We mustn't confuse a lack of material means with poverty. My father never stopped saying that dignity is the true wealth. He lived on only what the parents of the students at his Qur'anic school could give him and on his garden. He never demanded anything and never held out a hand to anyone."

Murmurs.

"It's true! Sada knows something about this. He's got someone to take after. His father, Mapaté Waar, whom you know—the boss of the 'Tamarind'"—smiling—"raised him like that. I'll come back to that later. Now let's get back to our charlatans. We've become their commodity. Not just here, but on the continental scale: don't give in to laziness and what comes easy! With the money that they collect on the pretense of 'helping' us, they live high on the hog. They're in the same bag as miracle workers, card sharks, those moneymen who multiply banknotes, who wreak havoc exploiting the gullibility of believers in the easy route."

Laughs.

A deep breath. Uncle Mbengue still, with his bright smile: "Sada's example should inspire us. His story at our school is a love story, a story of trust and gratitude. School, of course, offered him the opportunity to take this little step that makes us proud. The certificate in two years!"

Bursts of applause. Fervor and pride. They all know the story, having lived through it day after day. Before the "feat," Sada had become (without meaning to) the darling of the community. Not just the students. Gone was the time—the very short time, let it be said—of jibes about his age. Adored just as much by the teachers, the people outside with their stalls, and the lower employees. This salt-of-the-earth boy had impressed them all with his behavior that was so out of fashion at that time when disrespect for all people and all limits had become the norm.

Twice a week, he struggled to clean the establishment's large courtyard, to plant trees, to line Filaos in tight rows around the perimeter, to protect them with barbed wire. And to dig a well!

Yes, a well. Nobody had considered it since the water table was at least four meters deep. But the well was much needed: water shortages were a regular thing in the neighborhood; pestilential odors filled the atmosphere.

Little by little, the space changed its look. Sada, with his incredible magnetism, had ended up passing his enthusiasm on to the other students. All proud and happy to participate in the projects and to play in designated play spaces that were much airier than the dusty alleys of the neighborhood. Especially during school breaks, when the recurring floods dragged mud and refuse right into the houses.

The most beautiful gift he offered them was to infuse these innocents' hearts with the joy of sharing: to know how to give some of oneself and to feel deep inside the elation and the magic of a tiny seed sprouting, to tend to it, to accompany it all the way to the miraculous eruption of a stem. And to dream! That wasn't on the list of their worries. To dream . . . why not? Tomorrow, a forest . . . baobabs, Senegal mahoganies, acacias, palm trees, birds dancing, concerts at dawn under Sada's enchanted flute. "Like in paradise," Sada had told them.

"What Sada has done, you can all do," added Uncle Mbengue. "Don't let them come tell you, 'You're poor.' Poverty is not a foregone conclusion. I'm speaking particularly to the teens here and to the parents who no longer bother trying to forge in their children's hearts a tough shell of virtues—and who, in so doing, expose them to delinquency, to all sorts of wrong turns including suicide in those miserable pirogues. Your destiny is here! The solution to your troubles is within yourselves. It's up to you to make good use of the forces sleeping inside you! Bravo, Sada!"

Thunderous applause. A deafening din. Pause. Then: "Do you know how Sada managed to finance all these construction projects?"

Murmurs.

"I'll tell you. With the money he made from fiddling around building miniature objects: cars, pirogues, musical instruments, even up to the flutes he uses to accompany the birds' early morning flight!"

Rich applause. Sada, sage as an icon.

"With the profits he regularly put into his family's store, he advanced himself the sum that allowed him to make good on his expenses, which at this point are all paid off."

This just slayed the crowd. Tears on Sada's cheeks. For once, he cried. Mapaté would never say to him, "A boy doesn't cry . . . " He would understand that his son had cried tears of joy and honor.

Uncle Mbengue in seventh heaven. The spirit of Mapaté's Tamarind had visited the school—for eternity.

The director, Uncle Mbengue, regularly stopped by Mapaté Waar's courtyard. Not as a simple spectator. A stakeholder, absolutely. Under the dome of the mythic tamarind tree whose leafy branches danced with the wind and toyed with the sky, he gave wise advice and courses on "lessons in things," as people said at that time to mean "earth sciences." For the simple pleasure of sharing and then repeating laughingly: "I didn't come up with anything! I learned to know life like each of us can do."

Then, he liked to invite his muses. Inspired poet, storyteller when he wanted, full-time philosopher. Author of essays on astronomy and mathematics, he had a bee's instinct and flitted cheerfully among the fine flowers of every civilization's spirit and imagination. All this to say, the man was a walking encyclopedia. With an ease and a generosity that dazzled.

Later, when the time would come for him to retire, he would be named an ambassador and would honor his obligations with dignity. He would be called upon frequently as a mediator, to wade full bodied into the tumultuous and sometimes bloody waters of the conflicts that peppered the continent. He would not lose himself, thank goodness. And he would pursue, right up until the end of his long life, his quests into the unfathomable universe of the mysteries of civilizations and nature (his passion up until his last breath).

Adouna dafa goudou tank, life has long legs. Sada too. Between the fields, crafts, and training schools. Across forests, savannas, and hills. He traveled the length and breadth of the country. He set up corner stores in suburban zones born of cities' overflow. Quickly sprung from bare earth, new neighborhoods popped up like mushrooms. With no zoning plan or any kind of infrastructure. Not even evacuation routes. Sand, clay, or laterite, depending on the ground in each spot, had to take on garbage and sewage until it flooded over. The sun and the wind took care of the rest.

Even still, some nicer and airier spaces did the job for some who were not rich by any means but knew how to make ends meet with a resourceful can-do spirit and a lot of ingeniousness. Sada's got flair. Advised by Taaw, he quickly understood the benefit in developing in these areas far from city centers a chain of convenience stores that would be better organized than the usual "informal" boutiques traditionally plunked on street corners or tacked on to the front of people's houses.

The example of his family's store expertly run by Taaw inspired him. Starting from Mapaté's once-uncertain bric-a-brac, it had prospered. In a few years, it had transformed into a large store providing food and construction items.

After getting Mapaté a lease on the parcel of land they'd been occupying since they settled at the dump, Taaw thought he should secure the land with a deed—the only solution to save the area around the Tamarind and Mapaté's shack. "The

Courtyard," in short. For the symbol it represented, beyond its merely geographical contours.

A long ordeal in the dark channels and labyrinths of laxity, real estate fraud, and corruption. Slimy government workers sold titles legally acquired by honest citizens without incurring the least sanction.

Taaw had seen it all. Missed meetings, sullen faces, grating rudeness from agents who were incompetent and sometimes aggressive. He put up with it. Zen and optimistic as always. Bravely choking down his setbacks.

Finally, his stubbornness paid off. One day, coming into the soulless office where he'd long been hanging around with no result, he had the agreeable surprise of being received by a freshly recruited agent in his thirties. The young man greeted him with courtesy, inviting him to take a place at a small rectangular table, facing him. He listened attentively before getting up. Against three walls of the office, metal cabinets streaked with rust. He went on the offensive against drawers that frankly resisted, emitting groans that grated Taaw's ears. Time goes by ... The task proved difficult, but the young civil servant continued to scan cardstock folders whose mangled labels made it impossible to guess the contents of the dossiers. Taaw started to feel uneasy. Impatience? A knot in his throat. He heaved a great sigh to get it out. Time goes by ... Taaw began to doubt ... This was not part of his usual range of feelings. He, solid as a rock! Zero problems since "Bougouma" faded into the junk heap of oblivion, for eternity. Here he is, wrestling with an anguish that's gripping him. Taaw! He who had scraped the bottom of the pot of all the miseries of the world and come out unscathed ... by dint of his intelligence and his ability to resist in the face of adversity. But, above all, thanks to the sublime light that one day, at the shadowy dawn of a day that started out badly, guided his steps to the "paradise" he could never have dreamed of.

Paradise: Mapaté and Sabou's modest shack, facing a mountain of garbage and the constant rumbling of dump trucks. That modest shack had changed his life because there, he had found love and generosity, which in themselves have the virtue of reviving the sleeping soul of the damned.

Here's Taaw thinking again, "Maybe our dossier got lost. What if I, as the eldest, am not able to safeguard our family's estate?!"

And then, his eyes misty, no longer even looking at the young government worker struggling with his drawers and the files piled up on the floor: "The key is not that perishable paper. A deed can get ripped up . . . we can try elsewhere . . . Now, honor—that's another story! To rip that up is to die from the disdain of those we respect." And then he hears with terror in his shredded conscience the sentence that certainly wouldn't come from Mapaté, Sabou, Sada, or all the other well-meaning and well-educated people. It would come from jealous, bitter, cruel spirits: *Doo Darra*! You are nothing! A sentence of failure and degradation.

You never know when and how the capricious Ocean will vomit up to the surface all its bitter rejects.

It's like that with life: there are events and memories that rattle around throughout our existence. They can show up with no notice. Like that attack organized by a gang of hoodlums who'd burned down Taaw's neighbor's house in the middle of the night; at the time he was living in a modest room he'd built in the courtyard behind the store, with permission from the landlady, who hadn't asked for any increase in rent. Taaw's respectful attention and consideration were eminently sufficient for her.

The hoodlums and their bosses had justified their attack with the fact that the owner of that three-story building wasn't really from the area. That, having arrived penniless, he was showing off like a nouveau riche upstart, waving his wealth in everyone's face. And that the land on which he'd built his building belonged to their great-grandparents. And that the beneficiary—their uncle—now couldn't rub two cents together and had lost his mind.

Taaw had received a rude awakening whose effect he'd underestimated, classifying the event in the category of the fights and other "ordinary" violence that marked the tempo in certain neighborhoods. Nobody had reacted. Not the political or administrative authorities, not those in the neighborhood—nobody. Even though the building owner waved his deed around anywhere and everywhere the law might have counted for something.

Lost in the whirlwind of his nightmares, Taaw didn't even realize that the worker was coming toward him, a manila folder in his hands, staring wide-eyed as he sat down across from him.

"Mapaté Waar . . . from Les Filaos . . . the Courtyard, the Tamarind? Is that the right one?"

"That's him," responded Taaw with serenity, trying to escape the confusion that was gnawing at him.

Visibly moved, the government worker revealed: "I knew the Courtyard. Fascinated by that giant tamarind like none I'd ever seen. Such energy there—the stories and legends . . . the 'Old Man,' his unique way of picking apart proverbs. And his magical, intoxicating voice . . . so beautiful you couldn't believe it could be so charming, at his age. When he started in on the poetry of the *bakk*, the wrestlers, dancing happily . . . despite how rickety he was. Right now, as I'm talking to you, I feel like I'm transported right back there. I am there. Not to mention Uncle Mbengue's off-the-cuff riffs. Better than what we'd learn in class."

Silence. Then: "Uncle Mbengue was my teacher my first year at school, before he became the principal."

Taaw left him all the time he needed to pour his heart out. Memories, emotion, nostalgia . . .

"Does the Courtyard still exist? And what about the 'Old Man'?"

"Yes, it's still going, under the direction of the 'Old Man,' who gets younger every day God makes."

"*Al Hamdulillah!* Thanks be to God! Peace in heart and soul—it feels great to hear that!"

"For sure . . . "

"I left the area when my father was assigned to Ndaar Guedj," said the young man. "Saint-Louis . . . a real paradise!"

"How so?"

"I can't explain. Everything moves you there. It's in the air, the trees, the river."

"Are you married?" Taaw asked him.

"Not yet."

"I bet you it'll happen in Ndaar, with a Saint-Louisian woman."

"Certainly!"

Surprised by the apparently reserved young government worker's enthusiasm, Taaw burst out laughing before going on: "Did you know Sada, my younger brother?"

"Oh, yeah! He was our 'Big Guy': kind, available, hard- · working."

After the trip down memory lane, he asked Taaw to come back ten days later. Ten days later, the precious document was waiting for him on this atypical government worker's table.

Blessed deliverance! And Taaw cried out: "*Taaw da fa ka nourou.*"[9]

---

9. "An eldest son must be worthy of such a title."

"An angel in the crocodile swamp!" thought Taaw, picking up the document. He thanked the man warmly.

"My name is Bara Diop. I will come back to the Tamarind. Please give my respects and all my affection to the 'Old Man.'"

In a few months, the landscape had changed around the Tamarind. Three little houses cheekily planted in the scene. The parents' was where the former shack had been, big enough to house the "girls," as they were affectionately called in the family before they were married. It had been ages since they'd moved out to start their own homes, Dior in the rice fields of the south, Siga along the lagoons of the Petite Côte. They regularly made trips to Les Filaos to savor the incomparable sweetness and cohesion of the family cocoon. Sabou's smile, Taaw and Sada's teasing—and Mapaté's stories.

A little house for Taaw, his wife, and their two children. Up until then, he'd lived in an apartment, his little room in the back courtyard of the store having been expanded to house his wife and kids.

The third reserved for Sada. Still single, he spent more time wandering around.

The whole thing forming a miniature "compound" ringed in by a eucalyptus and Jerusalem thorn hedge.

Taaw in seventh heaven when the project was done. He never got tired of ragging Sada at each of his "layovers."

"An impregnable fortress, eh, little brother? Things are changing for the worse in these neighborhoods. Security has become a priority. Reassuring for everyone, no? Even for you, the eternal traveler, to know we're safe."

Impish smile from Sada, knowing the old refrain would follow, Taaw's signature farewell to him: "Little brother, you've really got to start thinking about getting married!"

Sabou didn't hold back from backing Taaw up: "Sada, Taaw is perfectly right. Single till when? The girls are married!"

Bursts of laughter from Sada.

"*Yaaye Boye*,[10] the girls are married, and good for them. Girls are always rushing to get married. I'll think about it, *InshAllah*, when God decides I should."

Sabou cut him off, her index finger aimed right at Sada's nose: "*Hiii! Yalla Yalla Bey sa toll!* Help yourself and heaven will help you!"

Laughter.

"*InshAllah*, I'm looking for the ideal wife."

"Sada, don't be dumb. The ideal wife—what's that?"

Mapaté, tossing in his inevitable two cents: "The ideal wife . . . dash it! The double of your mother, of course!" And he started to sing Sabou's praises while beating the tempo:

The ideal wife, beautiful like Sabou,
Sweet like Sabou,
Generous like Sabou,
Spirit galore,
Jealous like no other . . . but generous.
The one I love,
Woman of the sun in my midnight dreams,
Mysterious like the Ocean.

Thus crooning the refrain of his initiation homework from so long ago, when his grandfather had asked him to write a secular text based on his Qur'anic studies before letting him loose in the jungle of the world.

All hearts singing with joy. Absolutely!

They would wait. Sada would continue to travel around, but when it came time for religious or traditional celebrations, he would never skip putting together a family "caravan," with the

---

10. "My dear mother."

whole extended family and some friends, for a joyous trip down to the village, to spend a week there and to come back to Les Filaos before leaving once again.

That day! The dizzying immensity of a distant land in the middle of nowhere. In the restaurant of the hotel where Sada set up shop when his business called him there. He glanced at last night's newspaper, which arrived in the early morning in this faraway region.

Waiting to be served. Here, they know his habits, his tastes, and the charming love of good food that perhaps forged his jovial, generous, courteous character. A man without complexes.

Pretty soon, there in front of him, a big bowl of porridge. A magical scent. And colors permanently etched into his DNA. The thin layer of palm oil on top of the velvety paste made from the flour of "souna" millet, that young, green grain of his dreams. Intoxicating wafts of steam that, any and every day, wherever he might find himself, transport him right back to the heart of the family cocoon. A miraculous detour that gives him energy and well-being.

He emptied the bowl quickly, like always, but that didn't prevent him from savoring the pleasure of it. And then he picked the newspaper right back up. On the front page, a quarter-page photo; next to it, another photo of a book cover: *Shame on us! What have we done with what we've learned?* The author: Mignane Sonko.

Something clicked in Sada's head. Since the separation, that sad day, in the house where the huts floated in a swamp of muddy water and filth, he hadn't ever met a single other person named Mignane. Strange! In a country where it's so typical to use the same names over and over. And look: a Mignane pops up here all of a sudden . . . in a photo, on the front page of the newspaper . . . as if chance doesn't exist and providence is never by accident. Mapaté always thought so: "Providence is a good sign, it speaks!" he would say.

"Here, at the other end of the world," thought Sada. In the early morning, yes . . . in the early morning! At the time when Sabou, that generous mother, would give out bowls of porridge to Mignane, Boly, and other kids, each one hurrying to receive his share before disappearing into his hut. And now, here pops up the reignited memory of an invigorating sequence of their life together all that time ago.

The photo! Dare he look for kid-Mignane's chubby face behind this well-shaven head, those lively eyes, those flat cheeks?

The title: **Shame on us! What have we done with what we've learned?** An attention-grabber. It rings like a punch to the chest. How to find out more? The publisher's name? No reference to it in the article inside the newspaper. "To get in touch with someone from here"—that's difficult. Shaky telecom network in this area. Except for the investors who run immense mining concessions. Gold and copper in abundance in this region. Their zones are full-on territorialized and enjoy all possible commodities where materials and means of communication are concerned.

Five years ago, Sada was able to grab a modest domain and had built up a team of gold panners from this country who knew the region and the ground layers well. He had them take extra training courses using online modules. "I can't make you into engineers, for I am not one myself. That said, I've managed to absorb the minimum."

"No *taff taffal*," Mapaté always said: "You can't just do whatever without knowing where you're going."

Uncle Mbengue would back that up later: "Don't deprive yourself of trying to understand the ins and outs of any activity you'd like to take up."

Sada had thoroughly taken in his mentors' lesson. Up until then, he'd never crossed over into investor territory. How could he learn more about that story? He kicked his audacity into high gear. He went to knock on the door of a company where he'd never set foot: "Hello, sir."

"Hello, Mr. Waar. Come in. My name is Léon."

Sada, surprised but reassured. "How on earth did this gentleman know who I am? I don't think I've ever met him," he said to himself.

Actually, he's not so naive that he doesn't know that "those people"—which is what people call them to underscore their reflex of picking up on the least movements of those around them—"those people" had gotten him on their radar a long time ago. They know everything about everyone. They have a knack for probing with their bare eye the innards of the earth just based on the color of the sand and granite before "going in" with an unheard-of violence to extract the riches so jealously incubated in the unfathomed depths, hidden in unthinkable galleries, alas destroyed by the voracious appetite of the human race. The madness of destruction, annihilation, and possession has snapped the umbilical cord that links our destiny to that of the world that surrounds us.

Before investing in this sector, Sada set his own limits. Knowing that nothing could keep him from staying himself, imbued since forever with that intoxicating empathy that has always oriented his actions and fed his passion for nature.

Léon welcomed him into his office. At the entrance, four rustic chairs in sculpted wood with beige cushions in the style of the local artisans. The computer on a large table and the whole arsenal of IT equipment. Sober, pleasant. A big bay window and views as far as the eye could see.

"What can I do for you, Mr. Waar?"

Sada, from the get-go: "Here"—unfolding the newspaper before his host's eyes—"it might seem stupid to bother you for such a little thing. But I'm trying to find this book. As you can see, there's no information about the author, except his name, nor even about the publisher. You know the difficulties of the network around here."

Friendly smile from Léon. "We'll try . . . "

His fingers already on the keyboard. Two or three minutes . . . five tops, problem solved. It was Léon's wide grin that let Sada know. The book was published in France. The author: Mister Mignane Sonko, water and forestry engineer, agronomist, professor at the School of Earth Sciences. "Wow!" he exclaimed. "You know him?"

"I just might. I think I knew him when we were children. How can I order that book?"

"It's in stock at three bookstores in Dak and in a bookstore at the Ziguinchor Airport."

"Zig?"

"That's what the press release says."

"How can I order a copy?" repeated Sada.

"It's done, Mr. Waar. I've ordered two, to treat myself. I'll treat you too. This might interest me. We're expecting a delivery tomorrow, and I'll have it dropped off at the hotel. It's the hotel Bentannier, right?"

Sada, very moved: "Thank you so very much, sir—"

"Call me Léon."

"Thank you, Léon."

Shame on us! What have we done with what we've learned?
Everyone's been talking about it since the Western press gave the book abundant coverage, following an article full of praise for it in a prestigious French newspaper. Mignane hadn't hoped for so much. Never had any pretense of being "crowned" a writer. "It's enough for me to be what I am, to practice and teach the fields I've studied, to listen and to try to understand

all the whispers of all the worlds. And to allow myself to say out loud what I really think."

That's exactly what he'd said to Massamba, one of his schoolmates he'd met at university in France. For years, their conversations had founded and strengthened the basis of a friendship that would survive forever—even when Mignane decided to go back to his country at the end of his studies, his head full of projects, hope slung over his shoulder along with his bags.

It was to Massamba that he'd sent the text—not to publish it, but to spark questions, arguments, and reflections, as was their custom together.

Massamba had mailed the manuscript to the publisher without notifying Mignane. Knowing him to be ridiculously meticulous, he feared an outright refusal that he couldn't in good conscience override, out of respect. Might as well present his friend with a fait accompli and, worst case scenario, bravely swat away Mignane's reproofs.

The publisher—one of the "biggies" of the field—responded unequivocally. Yes to publication. Intoxicating joy in Massamba's heart: even though he was impressed by the text, he wasn't sure that that publisher would deign even to glance at this "disjointed satire," in Mignane's own words. He allowed himself the pleasure of sending Mignane a telegram: "Dear friend, I won my bet. You had the courage to say—and say well—what so many people think without daring—or being able to—say. We're all involved!"

On the patio of a major bookstore, the reading and book signing attracted a big crowd. The university in all its parts, stereotypical "intellectuals," "consultants," "analysts" present at all the debates that set the tempo of the Nation. Also: respected personalities, more or less well-known to the wider public, educated men and women who still practiced that old-school religion of acquiring and respecting knowledge—the adepts of those thousand ways, since the beginning of time, to access the various channels and forms for transmitting the history and culture of peoples and civilizations. *Adouna dey dox*, the world keeps going; *Adouna dafa goudou tank*, the world has long legs. To know where one comes from and who one is: the royal road to forging a sense of belonging to Humanity in all its most valorizing aspects. While still cultivating the garden of our myths, ideals, and utopias on the sanctified edifice of our values. In planetary complicity with "all the whispers of all the worlds."

Massamba had estimated that, even just for these words, what Mignane had to say needed to be heard, our globalized world being in desperate need of relearning the virtues of love, tolerance, justice, dialogue, generosity, respect, and—above all!—dignity.

Among these men and women: retired and active teachers, bookworms who were happy and proud of it, nostalgic for an era of rigor and high standards in virtue and dress.

Sada present, of course. For having had—again—the luck and audacity to have sniffed this out before others had. Léon decided to go along with him. A chance for him to tell a scrap of his story. Originally from the north of France. At the time, his parents were teachers in a high school: his mother taught math; his father, English. They went back to France the year he got his high school diploma. A faultless college career, then back to the country of his childhood. Recruited by the mining company where Sada had found him.

Sada approached Mignane. He displayed all the airs of a "personality" imbued with his own importance. Serious face. Handshakes. Sada, looking right in Mignane's eyes. Mignane's hand in a vice grip. Mignane, his eye fixed on the face of this colossus who doesn't let go. A staring contest. Silence around them.

"Hello, Mr. Sonko," said Sada with emphasis.

"Mister ... ?"

No response. After a short pause, sure he'd won the match, Sada spread out a wide smile.

"Sada! It's you! Sada!" cried Mignane. An emotional hug. Applause from the crowd.

"You're really something, my brother," said Sada, giddy as a kid.

"Where we're from, they say only a frog breeder can spot one that's limping! I won because your crafty kid's smile is permanently engraved on my memory's hard drive."

A great ambiance, a wave of emotion.

It's at that moment that Boly, third ruffian from their old group, arrived. After traveling the ninety miles from the village where he was teaching.

As it had for Sada, the first name Mignane had attracted Boly's attention when the event was announced on the radio. He had feverishly flipped through telephone directories without even remembering Mignane's last name and despite the fact that it had been thirty years since Mignane's father had gone back to his region to run a farm. That got him smiling to think: "It's funny, but except for at school—in the classroom—kids are only known by their first names. At the time, at home and even in the neighborhood, we were just Mignane, Boly, Sada."

A deep breath of tenderness.

And then he headed for the post office, where he called one of his cousins who'd lived in the same house. "That can only be our Mignane," the cousin had confirmed. "I remember well, the 'Old Man' was named Birima Sonko."

Abracadabra, after a relaxed hello and a wave to the whole room, Boly slid between Mignane and Sada, who spontaneously cried out, "Boly! Boly!" followed by the enthusiastic crowd.

Mignane explained in a few words what connected them all from a tender age, in a house where their parents were housemates from diverse origins, cultures, and affiliations. Where they'd never suffered from the modesty of their families' means, thanks to the generosity and love that brightened their destiny and made them find each other again, after so many years of separation, by the grace of God "around a book that I wasn't even expecting would be one. We're all involved! My friend Massamba said so. If we're together here this afternoon, it's his fault! Yes, Massamba's fault. Not mine."

Hearty applause.

After a word of welcome from the bookstore owner, Mignane went down the line signing books before responding with his characteristic sobriety to the audience's questions. In the front row of the audience, those ladies who were known to everyone as "the three twins." They were always together at the theater, the movies, in libraries and bookstores, at art exhibitions. In sum, at the cultural and artistic ceremonies they deemed worthy of their interest. Yacine, Coumba, Borso. In reality, Yacine and Borso were twins; Coumba, their childhood friend.

All three of them had gone to the same elementary school in the county where Mame Fara Diaw, the twins' father, was the district chief. They qualified to take the middle school entrance exam, which at the time was organized at the regional level. The most brilliant were sent to the most prestigious school set right in the heart of the capital. The catch: there was no dormitory for girls at that school. Coumba's parents had no choice but to sign her up for the all-girls' middle school, which was less cov-' eted. Mame Fara Diaw offered to have Coumba lodge, along with the twins, with his sister who resided in that beautiful ancient city of Ndar, the capital of the region. Coumba felt at ease there, a full-fledged member of the family. Six years later, they went off to university. Yacine studied geography and botany; Borso, classical literature and dramatic arts; Coumba, English literature. The two families, Mame Fara Diaw's and Coumba's parents, never separated. Henceforth joined for life.

Yacine, Coumba, Borso. Three firecrackers, strong personalities each in her own style.

Before closing out the event, Mignane having figured he'd said enough and preferring to let the book "speak" for itself, the bookstore owner turned to address the audience.

"Maybe a reading of two or three passages from the book?" All eyes turned to Borso. This whole crowd—or almost—knew her at least by name. She'd had the idea to set up in her courtyard a space for readings, debates, and conversation. One fine day, she decided to baptize it "the Empire of Illusion."

Coumba got up: "Borso!" The whole room chanted, "Borso! Borso!" Not to bother her. She even seemed happy to take on three passages from the book.

"Ladies and gentlemen, I feel honored to offer you three excerpts from Mr. Sonko's book. I could have written them myself if I'd had the author's talent."

Highlights: Excerpt I

Where is the world going? No values anymore! Most basic element of Love, cement of fraternity and peace. Humanity stripped of its nobility. Horror! All means acceptable for satisfying base instincts. Who's to blame? All of us who don't raise our children properly anymore, busy as we are chasing after honors and prizes.

We must compose ourselves. Or chaos straight ahead. We must rethink the meaning of our existence—in ourselves and with others. Humanity is one, with equal dignity, everywhere on the planet.

Banish hate, disdain, injustice, incredible cruelties. Sanctify the ideals of peace, solidarity. (Am I dreaming?) It's ever so beautiful to know from the bottom of one's heart the exhilarating light of goodness (does that word still exist?)—plain goodness, with no adornment or artifice, nor voyeurism, nor petty calculating. Hate wars that only serve to soil our land with the blood of cyclical massacres, always "negotiated" at a steep price.

Pray, pray, pray! When the inhibited conscience will spring miraculously forth from the ruins of our pride and turpitude, of our violence and voracity, it will speak to us.

Highlights: Excerpt II

Nothing counts anymore. Neither what is spiritually sacred—God, His Omnipresence in us, His Divine Light to guide the conscience—nor what is profanely sacred, what our ancestors of all the peoples of the world built on the base of inviolable values and principles to safeguard our dignity.

Today: the absolute ruler: money. The style in fashion all over the planet: illusion. Political illusion, industrial illusion. The chemistry that misleads and violates our absolute right to know: What food are we eating? What medicine are we taking?

The trend here: laziness. How to understand under our skies the mental indigence that blocks judgment and pride and incites people to gobble up the idea that we cannot make happen here, in our own homeland, for ourselves, what other peoples living in rougher geographical and climatic conditions have been able to make happen? Our well-being by the sweat of our brow! It's time to get going on that.

The supreme misfortune: renouncing the respect that each human being deserves to expect from their fellow human. The lack of self-esteem. We accept without shame to be classified as "the poor." For eternity? After God, our destiny depends only on our will to work. Funders, partners, investors . . . Is it logical that they "develop" us as we understand it and deprive themselves at the same time of the immense riches they rake in? An inspired poet once wrote in a poem that he was kind enough to give me: "Financial backers never let anything go behind their back!"

Highlights: Excerpt III

What good are the Humanities? I may as well have written: Should we murder Humanity? To hear honorable decision makers, teachers, scholars put up a hue and cry:

"We must privilege the scientific, mathematical, and technical sectors, for they alone can grant access to knowledge and know-how that is compatible with development: hard sciences and economics." Have they forgotten that their icons, the great scholars who revolutionized the world of mathematics, of physics, of chemistry, and of astronomy were also great philosophers, and thus concerned with the importance of the humanities? For the good reason that Man (Woman) is at the heart of the human adventure.

I remember hearing on the radio an eminent professor of medicine, a renowned oncologist. On the theme, "Why is medicine becoming dehumanized?" He nostalgically evoked the glorious epoch when the deep "self" of the students was not "fractured" into two false identities. One, the world of hard sciences; the other, the world of the humanities.

He lamented being in the last generation of literature BAs who turned to medicine.

Before, minds were trained to understand and digest the realities of the world in its rational, physical, concrete components and, at the same time, fed at the fertile springs of our history. Our spiritual quests, our doubts, our fears, our hopes, our anxieties, and, happily, our dreams, our emotions, and our follies. In a word: our capacity to transcend the universe on the planetary scale and to say with total sincerity: "My house is that sparkling star that shines in the sky; at the same time, it's my horse; in one second, it takes me all the way around the world, sets me in paradise, with the promise of bringing me back down to solid ground."

One can say all this without being disproven. Because the imagination is a thousand thousand times vaster than all the science and math books combined. Two plus two is four: no other possible outcome.

We were speaking about "Illusion!" Yes, Art in all its forms is illusion! Sublime illusion, which saves us.

So, stop force-feeding us with that same slogan of all math, all science, all economics. Besides, "all economics" has driven the world mad, mad, mad!

Art is illusion, yes! The only illusion that can heal us, a powerful neutralizing force against hates, hostilities, and pathological dumbing down.

Silence . . . silence . . .

"Come back to earth!" cried Borso. Bursts of applause.

She finished her act, smiling. Oh, her voice!

Every word, pause, or gesture has a meaning. Borso, herself.

Sada invited Boly and Mignane to Les Filaos, a chance to visit his parents and the family. This happened as soon as the following Sunday lunchtime. Sabou, beaming, displayed all the treasures of her heart to please "her children."

Generosity, love, joy. Sada introduced them to Taaw, "the eldest of the family," with his wife and children. No more said. Boly and Mignane didn't bother to try and find out more about this older brother they hadn't known at the time.

Emotion and marvel when Sada walked them through his storybook: the dump, Mapaté Waar's Tamarind and the Courtyard, school and Uncle Mbengue. A visit to the bird park. A tour along the lakeshore. A visit to the store. The family estate, in short.

Truly charmed by this "little paradise," the luxurious greenery and the revitalizing airs of the atmosphere, Boly and Mignane in turn expressed their pride and their deep gratitude, without forgetting to emphasize the courage, self-denial, and sacrifices needed. And to recall the millet porridge that Sabou served all the kids of the household.

"*Hii!*" exclaimed Sabou with tenderness. "You remember."

"Obviously! *Yaaye*, Mom!"

Mignane, usually a man of few words, addressed Sada, the whole family listening: "Sada, what I dream of in my book, you have made happen. You could have written that book to narrate, without pride or bragging, the story of a life of self-sacrifice, courage, labor, and success. The story of a conquest, a victory over life's difficulties that can be overcome by work, energy, and the absolute desire to succeed. To address the challenges that inevitably come our way. Eternal lamentations, the hand held out, and mental and physical laziness lead nowhere."

To wrap up, a show with songs, stories, and fables, under the Tamarind before a dazzled audience. In crescendo, Sada's flute meandering in the graying veils of the lowering sun to accompany the birds on their journey home.

That day, they made the unshakable decision to stay in touch.

As soon as Boly and Mignane left in the latter's vehicle, Sada headed straight to Taaw's house.

"Hey, big brother! Eureka!"

"What?"

"I told you I'd been looking!"

"Looking for what?"

"The ideal woman!"

"Are you pulling my leg or what?!"

"I'm not joking, big brother. Her name is Yacine Diaw. She and her twin, Borso, and Coumba Diagne make a trio that everyone calls 'the three sisters.' I made their acquaintance. Not really. More like I ran into them at the Xam Xam[11] bookstore during Mignane's book signing."

"So, what makes you say that she's the ideal woman?"

"My gut feeling. You yourself and lots of other people tell me that time and again!"

11. "Knowledge" in Wolof.

"Be serious!"

"I'm not joking, I promise."

"Have you talked to her already?"

"No. Really, I didn't dare."

It's true. He didn't have the guts, for once—he couldn't bring himself to broach the subject with Yacine. That said, he'd taken measures not to lose sight of her when the audience, in packed rows, hurried toward the bookstore's exit. He caught up with the "three sisters," Mignane, and Boly, who were obviously waiting for him so they could all say goodbye.

Congratulations to Borso for her performance.

Sada's nerves ablaze while shaking Yacine's hand. The sulfurous smell of a flash. A photographer appeared out of nowhere. Doubtless, the last of the pack of wandering photographers who hunt down any ceremonies they can find. His flash fires off. The group in full. Sada between Borso and Yacine. Coumba between Boly and Mignane. Sada, his heart racing. Yacine luminous, impenetrable, the littlest trace of a smile at the corner of her mouth. Her eyes . . . oh, her eyes!

Scrolling through the images right in front of Taaw:

"There she is! That's her. What do you think of her?"

"Let me look first. She's beautiful. No doubt about it. She looks grounded . . . intelligent . . . She's got character, for sure."

"Listen, big brother! I didn't know you were adept at these sciences. My only interest is to marry her!"

Taaw burst out laughing.

"*Gnaw!* It serves you right that after so many years of bumming around, this woman drives you crazy!"

The marriage was held a few months later with great pomp. When Sada Waar, the great-grandson of the honorable Serigne Modou Waar, and Yacine Diaw, the daughter of Mame Fara Diaw, unite "for better," that gets people moving.

From all over the country, delegations flocked under the tent set up in the vast courtyard of Yacine's parents' home—for the party that was naturally grandiose, but above all, because each and every guest felt the sacred duty to play their role. Weddings are a crucial moment when the community in all its different parts comes together around a ritual ensuring the continuation of their sacred bonds of loyalty to History. An opportunity to reenliven their heritage.

Before the event, Mame Fara Diaw and his family, thoroughly jarred by the incredible abuses that threaten each day to ruin the country right down to its roots, decided to take a few precautions.

Mame Fara Diaw invited Sada to a discussion of the conditions around organizing the wedding, in the presence of the twins and Coumba. Faithful to his reputation as a man of honor, with a delicious courtesy, respectful, affable, debonair when he wanted to be, he chose to tease Sada.

"So, young man, you want to take my daughter!" Enough to relax the atmosphere and put everyone at ease, especially Sada, strongly intimidated by Mame Fara Diaw's stature. And then the latter smiled: "You see, my children, it's the best thing a parent could wish for their progeny. To found a household, a partnership for the long haul. Trust, love, respect . . . on those fronts, I'm not worried."

Silence.

"I know my daughter . . . my daughters!" His finger pointed to all of them.

Laughter.

"We have every reason to trust you . . . to think of you as our son."

Silence.

"Sada, as you have been able to observe, money has ended up rotting people's hearts and the whole social fabric with very few exceptions . . . here and elsewhere . . . a human catastrophe."

Silence. Then: "I've thought about this for a long time. I've decided that, if I have to marry my daughters off, the dowry will be purely symbolic. Just the modest sum the mosque requires. I've been talking it over with my daughters for quite some time now . . . I'm thrilled to know that we're on the same wavelength. Thank God," he added, all smiles, looking at the girls.

Silence. Their eyes fixed on Sada.

"That's all, my son—except that I want to add—being basically persuaded this will never happen: in our family, we do not insult women, we do not hit them, they have the right to speak in all the couple's affairs. Whatever one might say now."

Sada, bruised on the inside, his head shaking side to side: "That will never happen, my father."

"I know, my son! I know where you're from. But, better to say it out loud, once and for all. So as not to have to say, 'If that ever happened,' 'I knew it,' or 'I saw it coming.'"

Sada had heard his father, Mapaté, say the same thing a thousand times.

"If you'd like to add a few words, my son . . . "

"I've understood it all, my father. Nothing to add. A real pleasure to listen to you. Your frankness dazzles me. With time, you will see that our families share the same values."

Mame Fara Diaw turned his gaze on the girls: "Yacine, as for you. Oh! I'm better off stopping myself from stepping on Yaaye Diodio's toes," he said with a debonaire tone.

A joyful rush. So lovely, so sweet.

Yaaye Diodio drank from the same source as her spouse and made it a point of honor to take care of transmitting that way of being to her children. Everyone knows she is dazzlingly

generous. Born to give, to share, to comfort morally and ma-
terially as much as she can. With absolute discretion.

That said, when circumstances require, she never holds back
from showing firmness.

Her sister-in-law, the *badiène*, or paternal aunt of her children,
showed up at the house two days after the conversation about
the marriage.

Routine visit.

Yaaye Diodio finally had the chance to get even with the
"*badiène*." That's what they call her at the house. For the simple
reason of being Mame Fara's sister, she thinks she's endowed
with a divinely granted authority: to intervene in family affairs,
to dictate her own laws to the children, to be spoiled with gifts
and simpering all the time. Yaaye Diodio never accepted this,
not giving two cents for her pouting, not ceding any of her own
rights and prerogatives as the responsible spouse, worthy of
being respected on all fronts.

She announced the good news to the *badiène*.

In front of the twins: "A young man named Sada Waar has
delegated members of his family to ask for Yacine's hand."

The *badiène* in seventh heaven.

"*Hamdulillah!*"

And there she went, stammering effusively through prayers
and good wishes for the future bride and groom.

"Who are the young man's parents?"

"I know he's the great-grandson of Serigne Modou Waar, a
great scholar known beyond the frontiers of his region and of
the continent. Mame Fara discovered in the colonists' 'papers'
the glorious story of Serigne Modou Waar and his ancestors."

"And as far as the dowry, the *warougard*, is concerned?"

"Mame Fara and all of us, including Yacine herself, don't
want a dowry. He told the delegation that there would not be
a dowry."

Yaaye Diodio intentionally stressed that point.

"No transaction, no bargaining, no festival of banknotes in *battré*.[12] None of any of that. Nothing but the modest sum of fifty thousand francs for the mosque. And, naturally, mineral water, cookies, candies, cola . . . all given out at the mosque."

"*Hiiii!*"

The *badiène* was completely disoriented. Dazed.

She cried out: "So basically, Yacine is offered up in sacrifice! We are part of the family, and in these circumstances, we have—we, the paternal family—a thing or two to say!"

Yaaye Diodio, like a marble statue.

The *badiène* got louder, her voice raspy.

"I'll talk to Mame Fara. He doesn't have the right to exclude us. Who's ever seen such a thing! We have a role here, not by the will of Mame Fara or anyone else, but by the Will of God. By the ties of blood. Family bonds are sacred!"

Yaaye Diodio left her all the time she needed to vomit out her anger before replying serenely:

"The family bond has no sense unless it rests on the sacred pillars of *yermandé*, of solidarity, of love, and of decency. Don't you forget it! We here certainly haven't."

Seized with emotion.

"We will never forget!"

A moment to dry her tears.

"We will never forget! How could we forget! When God called back to His fold my two twin boys, our eldest. In the flower of their youth . . . two years apart to the day, one after the other, Waly and Yalli. And desolation reigned here.

"Waly gone without so much as a peep. And then, quickly 'recovered' from your cries and lamentations, you made the rounds of your friends, acquaintances, community rainy-day

12. "To toss banknotes up in the air."

fund partners, and members of all different associations. And then you carved out here, in this big courtyard, a space all to yourself, to receive in return the sums that you had given in similar circumstances. A sort of business capital!

"Not a single member of my own family engaged in that macabre game over the corpse of a loved one. A youth, barely out of adolescence."

"*Hiiiii!*"

"Let me finish, please. Two years later, for Yalli's funeral, you wanted to start that up again. You must at least remember that two of Mame Fara's nephews came, on their uncle's orders, to announce the end of the funeral celebrations by piling up the chairs and folding the mats that you'd taken care to spread around 'your perimeter.' You insulted them left and right. You must remember that."

The *badiène* got up, headed toward the door.

The shadows of Waly and Yalli in the air. Fog in their hearts.

She got up and left. Her cheeks puffed with rage. Clearly not daring to engage in a fight with Yaaye Diodio, nor to toss insults at her, as was her habit.

The *badiène* is actually the adopted daughter of Mame Fara Diaw's mother. Her mother having died in labor in the heart of the Waalo, she was taken in by Mame Fara's mother. She integrated into the family to such a point that, in the course of things, she could take advantage of being a full-fledged member of the family. That was typical, given the values and customs of the time.

The only downside was that "more Catholic than the pope," she took it too far—in all the wrong ways—unlike Mame Fara's birth sisters, known for their physical elegance, their finesse, and their intelligence.

On the wedding day, she showed up. Serene, smothering Yaaye Diodio—and the bride—and also Borso and Coumba—with self-serving praise.

Borso, deep down inside, blocked her indignation.

"A sign of the times. Hypocrisy, you've really got us!"

After careful reflection, Sada made the decision to sell off his gold-mining concession. The zone was so out of the way, and travel was difficult, often on steep, rough, unpredictable roads.

Henceforth, father and head of household. Confronted with new obligations. Yacine and Borso were called back to their childhood home for professional reasons. Well, really, the affectionate pressure of the family (Yaaye Diodio and Sabou above all, but also Youma, Taaw's adorable wife).

"Bring us Diéry! Our little bit of a man . . . we want to feel him in our arms." The countless photos of the "little bit of a man" that brighten up their cloudiest days and light up their dreams aren't enough.

Sada sees the future through rose-colored glasses. Or, really, through gold-colored ones. The terms of the transaction briskly handled by Taaw allow him to realize his life's dream.

To put the finishing touches on his program to modernize his village and other localities in his home region. Projects of vital interest are already up and running. Two schools, one Qur'anic in Arabic and the languages spoken in the area; the other, a primary school run on the prevailing academic standards; a maternity clinic equipped with an ambulance—what a boon! Wells here and there. To the great joy of Taaw, the designated moral authority of the family. Sole manager . . . he doesn't mess around with the proper way of handling accounts. He's proven himself.

Ready to take it to the next level. Solar energy for electricity and all the wells necessary for running farms and processing facilities, figuring they can count on Mignane's expert advice.

All this with one goal in mind: the community's autonomy, liberty, and dignity. At the same time, they've benefited from technical training and an intensive awareness-raising program on their own obligation to produce results. Each one, to the extent of their ability, must assume responsibility.

Objective: self-funding. "Nothing is easy," Sada would say to them with such gentleness that the message obviously went straight to their heart by the magical virtue of respect.

Totally unlike the pompous and sometimes arrogant speeches of the supposed "development aid agencies," or of politicians in search of an audience. Some years before, the residents of the village had sent them packing without throwing either stones or insults.

"Here," he'd told them, "with *foula* and *fayda*, determination and dignity, the potent weapons of sages since the beginning of time, we have never begged for our little scraps. Our ancestors have taught us to make a pact with our land. We give her our strength and our sweat. She feeds us, cradles us, and makes us dream. If tomorrow, laziness or inattention pushes us to sell off at a shameful price the energy and resources hidden deep down in us, we'll fall to the lowest point of indignity."

For miles around, everyone knew the fabulous story of Serigne Modou Waar, and many had heard tell of Mapaté Waar's Courtyard in Les Filaos. Some had even seen—or at least glimpsed—Sada's regular caravans on the occasion of the various traditional and religious holidays.

During her time in the mining zone, savoring the breezes that swept the sunny home surrounded by plants and flowers that Sada had planted there, enhanced by the decorative ponds and ringed by red-earth dunes, Borso never let herself get bored. Giving herself over body and soul to her role as "little mother" to Diéry. Love and tenderness for the dear baby she would call for life *sama taaw*, my eldest.

Early in the morning, Sada would drive Yacine to the Research Center. An immense complex. More like a village. Cloistered by wrought-iron gates, impregnable. Inside, imposing structures on stilts. It was in front of one of these structures that everyone called "quarters" that Sada would drop Yacine off. Like a hive. Numerous researchers from different horizons would cross paths there all year long: geologists, botanists, agronomists, anthropologists, mineralogists.

Not for a single moment had Borso thought she'd be taking on a burden by accompanying her twin sister on this voyage into the unknown. For the very simple reason that the theater lives in her and follows her everywhere. She had prepared her adventure with the baby on the way, even before his first wails. To break all chains and all borders. To initiate Diéry into the mysteries of the world (visible or hidden). To catch glimpses of fantastical twists and turns in the universe of spirits and wild beasts, the baby solidly attached to her back with the *mbotail* blessed by Yaaye Diodio.

She took as much pleasure in nurturing the baby as she had in developing the writing of a play that had been in workshop for a long time: *The Bride Was in Spare Parts*. The idea, in her mind, went along with her favorite theme: illusion, in its thousand declensions.

Like a good number of well-meaning people, she could have safeguarded her personal "territory" by joyfully skipping above the nauseating sewers of illusion without either getting dirty or losing her soul. With her conscience at ease.

Once disgraced, spit out, falling apart, considered the stinking mother of all the forms of moral decadence, deceptive illusion had slowly, gently, surely become anchored in people's everyday habits. A national and worldwide mental gymnastics. To the point that an ambassador from a great European power seemed quite moved by it when he expressed himself in a newspaper. Not any old one, either; the national daily, the government's own organ. He had generally expressed appreciation for his stay, brought up the country's enormous potential, saluted the human warmth and generosity of the people. With a whiff of emotion, he'd underlined the refinement and beauty of the women. Correcting himself to be more precise: "The beauty of the women . . . the authentic ones."

Borso had read the newspaper. Vexed to the core, to the point of not being able to digest for a long time what she'd perceived as a dishonoring insult. She felt personally implicated.

Because Borso is Borso. She can't hide behind her own good conscience and say, "That doesn't concern me." Artist by vocation. No doubt born to become one. Just as Yacine— her carbon-copy twin sister—was calm and reserved, Borso was a magnificent jokester, the life of the party from her tenderest childhood, spreading joy everywhere, "pestering" everyone, including one of her elementary school teachers, nicknamed "Madam Do-Re-Mi-Fa" right after their first music lesson. That seasoned educator was charmed by Borso, blown away by the way "the little one" dramatized her recitation lessons, so she'd had the bright idea to create a small school-activities group with Borso and a few other students in her class. She had thus succeeded in taming the class while encouraging them to whip up their imagination and to express themselves through free-choice creations: drawings, stories, skits.

Borso would never let go of that thread. Vocation revealed, destiny accepted. Theater. On the hunt for deceptive illusion in all its forms, even where no one expected it. Not to moralize. "Moralizing! Nope, that's not my vocation! Go look at school, where lessons on ethics and civic education have disappeared from the curriculum. Or in the families who have totally given up on their part. I'm doing it to have fun and to share the ineffable happiness of being absolutely free to take in a huge breath of air in the kingdom of innocence."

Already, when Yacine, Coumba, and she were in college, she had made Coumba her preferred target. Allowing herself to do so thanks to the great complicity that linked them.

"Coumba, I'd warned you. You had such a lovely color, a smooth face, fine features. You've ruined your skin. Your *xessal*[13] is catastrophic!"

"That's not your problem. Tastes and colors are not up for discussion! My *'xessal'* is my business. Mind your own beeswax! You don't even have the time to take care of yourself. You're always running, running. If that's what it means to be an artist, no thanks! All scruffy, poorly dressed . . . " And then she adds, winking at Yaaye Diodio: "To the great chagrin of dear Mom, *Yaaye Boye*! Look how beautiful Yaaye is. Right, Yaaye?"

Yaaye Diodio laughed at their interminable heckling and teasing but refrained from intervening, being sure that the very next instant they'd be sipping their *ataya* as if nothing had happened.

In the kingdom of silence where she now rests for eternity, she must be smiling, rejoicing at having planted the right seed and given her family love and good feeling as their inheritance.

The Sada-Boly-Mignane trio: reconstituted forever more since the unforgettable event of Mignane's book signing and the phenomenal success that followed.

Regular trips to Les Filaos. An invigorating breath of air. Mapaté's ever-more-delectable riffs and shows. The effervescence of the always-thrilled crowd. And above all, the most impressive: mealtime in the family homestead, the incredible vitality—luminous, magic—that Sabou gave off. Her aura! Inspired conductor at the head of a family where each played, · without a single false note, the tunes of love, conviviality, and generosity. Taaw naturally appeared as the temple guardian in everyone's eyes.

Boly and Mignane savored Sada's caravans over the lands of Serigne Modou Waar, the immortal ancestor. And they swore

13. "Skin bleaching."

never again to miss them. Happy and proud, beyond what Sada had told them.

"Extraordinary!" said Mignane.

"Bravissimo!" said Boly, congratulating Sada, his throat tight with emotion. Under his cranky exterior, he actually wore his heart on his sleeve.

A few months later, Sada and Yacine moved from the "little paradise" of Les Filaos to a more spacious villa lost in the middle of fields, baobabs, mango trees, and Senegal mahoganies as far as the eye could see. And a tamarind, to keep the legend going. They had Boly and Mignane over again for lunch. "To christen the new digs," Sada had said, laughing. Coumba and Borso were there, of course, like every Sunday, to keep Yacine company. Borso essentially came just for the beautiful eyes of Diéry, *sama taaw.*

Meal, jokes, remarks.

Then Sada went ahead and got up, solemnly addressing Boly and Mignane.

"Listen up, you diehard bachelors!"

Boly cut him right off: "Oh, give it up! How long has it been since you left the ranks?"

"A while now, after all! Besides, I know there's something afoot."

"What do you mean?" asked Mignane, with a little smile at the corner of his mouth.

"Serious things, desirable things. I'm in the know!"

"Oh yeah?"

"Of course! I'm the first to get myself hooked. Your turn will come, I'm sure! However stubborn you are, this will happen to you soon too."

Bursts of laughter.

"It's an honorable rank to be the first, no?" And then he kept going, more seriously: "What links us is very strong. Friendship, loyalty, sincerity. Yacine—Mrs. Waar, if you please!"

Bursts of laughter.

"Mrs. Waar has charged me with a mission concerning you. She—along with the whole household, of course—would like for us all to share lunch here every Sunday. This isn't the time or place to brag about her culinary talents—you'll appreciate them yourselves. The most important thing being not to eat, but to create an occasion to be together, to have fun, eternal kids that we are, to reflect on how the world is changing. To keep our lucidity and our liberty in the face of the underhandedness, usurpations, and untruths, or illusions—as Borso would put it—that are turning us into robots. Mignane, the other day you said that blind conformity in the ideological, economic, and even scientific realm was the greatest danger of our time!"

Simultaneously, Boly and Mignane approved, thanking Sada and the family.

"The story continues. This started long ago. From Mama Sabou and Yaaye Diodio."

"And the inside scoop, then?" tossed out Boly.

Sada wouldn't reveal his secret for another two months. His source: Taaw himself.

During the last caravan to the ancestral country, Taaw had said to him smilingly: "Little brother, have you noticed anything going on with Boly and Mignane?"

"What?"

"They're in love."

"*Ey?* Big brother?"

"Borso and Coumba too. My intuition and my experience are never wrong."

"That I can confirm. But who's in love with whom?"

"I can't tell you that. Borso has been paying a bit more attention to her appearance. She's more coquettish than usual, better dressed; still loud—we can't cure her of that, it's part of her charm. Coumba is still chic but less 'shock.'"

"*Ey,* big brother!"

"I'd guess Coumba-Boly, Mignane-Borso."

The future would prove him right. Boly and Mignane would confirm it. Of a common accord, the future brides and grooms, their parents, and their families made the choice of Serigne Modou Waar's lands to celebrate the marriage festivities. To show their gratitude to the community who, along with Serigne Modou Waar and Mapaté as sources of inspiration and with Sada and Taaw as natural leaders, raised high the torch of dignity by cultivating the seed of hope, for the honor and grandeur of the Nation. To each their own energy, their faith, their intelligence.

Borso would put off until later the launching of her play *The Bride Was in Spare Parts.* Done was her mocking, like Coumba, who in the meantime had gotten rid of the black and red patches on her neck and shoulders that had earned her some cruel remarks.

Current cosmetic fashion having gone past the stage of "false eyelashes, false hair, false nails," Borso figured she had to get with the times. She imagined a scenario that was far from being incredible: an innocent young groom discovers, on his wedding night, that his beautiful young bride had false everything: false butt, false breasts, false teeth, false . . . He runs off as fast as his legs can carry him, buck naked, yelling while crossing with wide strides the antechamber, where the young bride's paternal aunts wait for the infamous cloth "of virginity."

AMINATA SOW FALL is a Senegalese novelist whose work has received international acclaim (Grand prix littéraire d'Afrique noire, Prix International Alioune Diop, and Grand Prix de la francophonie de l'Académie française), most notably for *Le revenant* (1976), *La grève des bàttu* (1980), *L'appel des arènes* (1982), *L'ex-père de la nation* (1987), *Douceurs du bercail* (1998), and *Le jujubier du patriarche* (1998).

MEG FURNISS WEISBERG is a creative writer, visual artist, and scholar of comparative literature, focusing on Africa and on Africa's cultural relationships with the rest of the world.

For Indiana University Press

Emily Baugh, Editorial Assistant
Brian Carroll, Rights Manager
Gary Dunham, Acquisitions Editor and Director
Anna Francis, Assistant Acquisitions Editor
Brenna Hosman, Production Coordinator
Katie Huggins, Production Manager
Darja Malcolm-Clarke, Project Manager and Editor
Dee Mortensen, Original Acquisitions Editor
Dan Pyle, Online Publishing Manager
Stephen Williams, Marketing and Publicity Manager
Jennifer Witzke, Senior Artist and Book Designer